COWBOY CLASSIFIEDS

seeking
NANNY

JANICE WHITEAKER

Cowboy Seeking Nanny, Book 1 of the Cowboy Classifieds series

Copyright 2020 by Janice Whiteaker.
www.janicewhiteaker.com

All rights reserved. No part of this publication may be reproduced, stored in a retrieval system, or transmitted in any form or by any means electronic, mechanical, photocopying, recording, or otherwise without the prior written permission of the publisher and copyright owner except for the use of brief quotations in a book review.

First printing, 2020

CHAPTER ONE

"WHY ARE THERE so many horses?" Wyatt's shaggy dark hair blew in the wind as he stared wide-eyed out the open passenger's window.

"There's probably a lot of horse farms around here." Clara squinted up at the street sign dangling from the single traffic light in downtown Moss Creek.

Wyatt's head turned her way, brows coming together over his big brown eyes. "Don't they call them ranches?"

"Yes." Clara took a deep breath, struggling to get the air to move in a way that felt even a little relieving. "I believe they do." The drive here was wearing on her almost as much as the past twelve months.

"Why do they call them ranches?"

She watched as the cars passed, doing her best to sound relaxed. "I'm sure Mrs. Pace can tell us when we get there."

"You think she's like a grandma?"

Clara fought in another deep breath, trying to ease the tension that never seemed to leave her body. Answering questions should not be this big of a deal, even when the string of them never seemed to stop.

This year had been just as hard on her sweet little boy. He needed her to be the best mom she could.

Especially now that she was the only parent interested in being a part of his life.

Not that it was much different than before. Now it was just more official.

Paperwork and all.

"I think she's like a mom. That's why she needs a nanny." The light turned red, stopping the intermittent cars spaced just far enough she couldn't turn earlier. Clara eased her second-hand sedan onto the one-way cross street before glancing at the map displayed on her phone to be sure she was headed in the right direction.

"If she's a mom, then why does she need a nanny?" His question was so honest. So genuinely confused.

It calmed the unrest brewing in her belly. The fears she'd been harboring since packing up their belongings and moving them out of California and into a new state.

A new life.

Without a word of fight from her soon-to-be ex-husband.

"Not all moms are as lucky as I am." Clara shot Wyatt a smile as she reached across to squeeze his hand in hers as a lump formed in her throat.

He'd been through so much. The loss of his home. His way of life.

His father.

Twat that he was, it was still a loss.

"You think they'll have horses?" Wyatt was back to looking out the window, his hand still clasped in hers.

"I'm pretty sure they do." Clara glanced down at the gas gauge before checking the mileage left on their trip. It was going to be as tight as the constraints she had to keep on her bank account.

But until the twat finally signed the divorce papers, she was stuck with nothing since it turned out Richard was just as successful at manipulating the system as he was at manipulating women.

Including the one currently incubating his next child.

"I hope they have horses." Wyatt's free hand gripped the base of the open window letting in the warm Montana air. "You think they'll let me pet one?"

"Maybe." Clara's stomach squeezed as the number indicating the depletion of her gas tank dipped lower. "We have to be good guests, though."

"I know."

They'd been over it a hundred times on the long trip. While Red Cedar Ranch might be their new home, it was someone else's home first.

Which meant it was still better than the tiny one-bedroom they'd been sharing for the past year, pinching pennies in the hopes that Richard would finally realize he couldn't simply walk away from his responsibilities.

Clara's heart picked up as the number of miles remaining on her tank dipped to single digits. She'd been sure they had enough. Positive she could milk the last bit to get to Red Cedar Ranch then wait on her first paycheck instead of pulling any more money from her rapidly-dwindling account.

"How much farther?" Wyatt leaned to peek at the screen of her phone. "It says six more miles."

"Yup." Six miles to go on four more miles worth of gas.

But she was due a break. Hopefully this would be it.

Four miles later it became clear this was not the break fate owed her.

As the engine sputtered and died her heart sank, taking down all the hope she'd pinned on this opportunity. "Godddd—" Her teeth clenched tight as she caught sight of her son's wide eyes.

Clara pressed her lips together, cutting off the end of one of the many words she wanted to scream at the top of her lungs into the deserted space around them.

There was nothing in sight. Nothing useful anyway.

Just the mountains in the distance and grass and fences and pavement.

Clara closed her eyes.

This was fine.

Fricking fine.

She sucked in a lungful of hot summer air, gritting her teeth against the urge to wallow in the unfairness of it all.

"Someone's coming."

Clara snapped her eyes open. She twisted in her seat, looking down the road as she reached across to press one hand against Wyatt's chest. "Stay here." She climbed out and onto the shoulderless road her car currently occupied half of.

A gleaming red pickup with extra wheels on the back end eased toward them. A black dog with flopped ears hung out the window, his tongue dangling from a mouth that almost looked to be smiling.

He must be having a better day than she was.

Clara slapped on a smile as the truck slowed to a stop. "Hello."

The man in the driver's seat tipped up the front of his tan cowboy hat. "Ma'am." He leaned to peek toward where her gasless sedan sat. "Car problems?"

"Um." Clara rolled her lips together, hating that she was going to have to admit to running out of gas. "It's more of a user error."

The man chuckled, his smile revealing deep dimples and straight white teeth. "I've had a few of those myself."

Before she could ask if he had a gas can, the man was out of the truck and heading her way. He paused, boots scuffing across the pavement as he caught sight of Wyatt in the front seat. "Well, hey there." His dark blue eyes came Clara's way. "You wouldn't happen to be on your way to Red Cedar Ranch, would you?"

Clara glanced back toward the truck. It was brand new. Clean. Well-kept.

Did serial killers drive nice trucks?

She turned to give the man a once over.

He was tall and muscular. Handsome, but way too young for her to consider him anything more.

He didn't *look* like a serial killer.

"Damn." He clicked his tongue. "Don't tell my momma I didn't introduce myself first thing." He reached a hand her way. "Brett Pace. I believe my momma is who hired you."

"Your *mother* is who hired me?" She's spoken with Mrs. Pace more than a few times over the past month. Never once would she have guessed the woman was old enough for this man to be her son.

Brett's smile widened. "It's not me you're nannying if that's what you're worried about." He shot her a wink.

"Are you a cowboy?" Wyatt was up out of his seat, his head poked through the open driver's window.

"You could say that." Brett opened the door. "Come on out, partner. Let's get you and your momma someplace safe."

Wyatt immediately jumped out of the car, his attention focused on the open window of Brett's truck and the canine hanging out of it. "Is that your dog?"

"Sure is." Brett reached into the car, twisting the keys until he could roll up the windows, before pulling them free of the ignition. "You need anything out of here before we go?"

Did he just think she was going to pack her child up in his truck and let him drive them off to God knows where? "Can I see your driver's license?"

This man seemed to know who she was and why she was there, but getting murdered in the mountains of Montana would be a fitting end to the past year of hell she'd been through.

And the day already wasn't promising.

Brett studied her for a second. "You're not from around here, are you?"

"No." Clara held her hand out. "I'm gonna need proof you are who you say you are before I get in that truck." Mrs. Pace was a friend of the attorney who now had most of the money Clara managed to wrangle away from Richard, but that didn't mean this man actually knew her.

And she'd blindly trusted a man before.

Which is exactly what led to her standing on the side of a

deserted road in Moss Creek, Montana, next to a useless car packed with everything she and her son owned.

Brett reached into the back pocket of his well-worn blue jeans, pulling out an equally well-worn wallet. "Don't judge a man by what he looks like without his hat." He passed over the plastic rectangle. The same handsome face smiled out at her, his dark hair matted down close to his head.

The address listed matched the one she'd entered into the map app on her phone three days ago.

"Thank you."Clara passed the identification back. "Sorry to be so difficult."

The apology came before she could stop it.

He tucked it back into place. "Don't be. It's nice to see someone who doesn't know every damn thing I've done since I was born." Brett turned to the truck and whistled between his teeth. "Back seat, Duke." The black dog bounced around a second before doing a full spin and jumping into the back of the truck's cab.

Wyatt's brown eyes widened. "He listens real good."

"Sometimes." Brett opened the door, catching Wyatt with one palm as the little boy tried to jump in. "Ladies first, little man."

Wyatt didn't miss a beat. He backed away, tucking in close at Brett's side in a way that made her heart ache.

Her son wouldn't have a father to show him how to be a man.

Just a twat who couldn't be bothered to put any effort into the child he helped create.

Clara tucked her chin as she passed Brett. She was right in the open doorway when the ridiculous height of the truck stopped her in her tracks. "How do I get into this thing?"

"Reach right up there and grab the handle." Brett leaned in close enough his body almost brushed hers. "Get a foot in and climb."

Clara pushed up on her toes, managing to get one hand on the handle he pointed out. Getting her leg up was another thing altogether. She hadn't planned to climb up the side of a mountain of a vehicle today, and her knee-length sundress was not cut out to keep her poor child and her new boss's son from seeing the thong she wore under it.

Which meant she ended up dangling from the damn handle, hanging on for dear life like she might be able to hoist her entire body up and in with the strength of that one arm.

Brett's eyes skimmed down her body, the quick pass stopping at the hem of her dress. "I didn't really think that one through."

Without giving her time to prepare, he grabbed her waist and lifted her up and in, hefting Clara into the seat like she weighed nothing.

Somehow she managed not to yelp or flail around in surprise, so that could be counted as a win. Especially on a day like this.

"You're up, Little Man." Brett bent at the waist, locking his fingers together and holding them out. "Step up in there."

Wyatt grabbed the door and immediately punched his foot into Brett's hands, easily jumping into Clara's lap. Brett closed the door, holding one hand up for Wyatt to slap. "Good job."

"Thanks." Wyatt grinned as Brett walked around to the driver's door.

"How am I supposed to buckle us in?" Clara fought the

seatbelt as Brett opened his door, tipping his head inside to watch her with amused eyes.

"We're just going two miles down the road. I'll drive real careful."

She let the belt retract into place and wrapped her arms tight around Wyatt's waist, prepared to act as a human restraint should the need arise.

Wyatt's questions started the second Brett was seated. "Do you have horses at your house?"

"Yup. Lots." Brett had one hand slung over the top of the wheel, not paying any attention to the road as he answered every question Wyatt shot at him.

"Do you have more dogs?"

"Yup. And cats."

"Do you ride them?"

"The horses or the cats?"

Wyatt cackled. "You can't ride cats."

Brett draped one arm over the line of the open window, whistling while his truck ate up the last miles to Red Cedar Ranch. As they got closer, the basic wire fencing was replaced by split posts and rails. Cattle grazed in grassy fields, their coats shiny in the bright summer sun.

It was like a completely different world from the one she'd been in for the past ten years.

Hopefully that was a good thing.

A metal archway stretched across a break in the fencing. Brett slowed the truck and turned onto the thick gravel covering the lane leading to Red Cedar Ranch. Wyatt sat up a little taller on her lap. "Where's your house?"

"It's coming." Brett angled the truck around a sharp bend flanked on one side by a thick line of trees.

"Holy cow." Wyatt stared out the windshield as the tree line broke, revealing the first glimpse of their new home. "*That's* your house?"

"Yup."

Clara stared alongside Wyatt.

This wasn't a house. This was an estate.

A compound.

And it only got bigger the closer they got.

Brett pulled the truck to a stop, parking in a line of other, similar trucks before getting out and coming around to help Wyatt jump down. He held one hand out. "Need a hand?"

Clara eyed his offered palm. She'd been on her own for a year, and depending on someone for anything ever again left a sour feeling in her gut. "I'm okay." She grabbed the door with one hand and her dress with the other, holding onto both for dear life as she jumped out, the soles of her flat sandals not doing much to protect the bottoms of her feet from the bite of the rough gravel.

But she smiled through it. Just like she'd done a million times in the past year.

Fake it till you make it.

"Can I go see the horses?" Wyatt had definitely already forgotten all their talk about being respectful.

"I'm sure Mr. Pace has things to do." Clara gave Brett an apologetic smile she hoped made it clear she'd tried to teach her child how to act right.

"Actually, I have *nothing* else to do." Brett lifted his brows at Wyatt. "But you should probably ask your momma if it's okay for you to go see them."

Wyatt turned his big brown eyes on her. "Can I please?"

She'd been able to give her son so little of what he was

used to since the twat decided he wanted to trade her in for a younger model, stripping away all she thought her life would be.

Clara scanned the ranch. This was supposed to be their new home. It's what she told Wyatt. Promised him.

He deserved to feel at home somewhere again.

She gave him a nod. "Remember your manners."

She watched as Brett and Wyatt made their way toward a large red barn.

This was going to be a good thing. What they needed.

What she needed.

Clara scanned the property, her stomach tightening.

Was she supposed to go find Maryann Pace?

Wait here for Brett and Wyatt to come back so they could go get her car from the middle of the road?

"Shit." Clara allowed a rare slip of one of her favorite words and dropped her head back to stare at the sky.

Once again she was only half-prepared for the life she was stuck in.

"Can I help you?"

A deep male voice sent her spine straight and her head leveling out. Clara spun around to face the source of the voice.

Oh hell.

Brett was easy to brush off.

He was cute, but definitely young.

The man in front of her was not what any woman would call *cute*.

Not by a long shot.

Clara licked her oddly dry lips. "I'm looking for Maryann Pace."

The man's startling blue eyes held hers. "Can I ask why?"

She stood a little straighter under his unwavering gaze.

Fake it till you make it. "I have an appointment with her."

One dark brow went up, disappearing under the low line of his cowboy hat. "Do you now?" He took a few long ambling steps her way. "Are you the interior designer?"

"What?" Clara glanced around the dusty fields and rocky drive. "No."

The man's head tipped a little. "Are you from the magazine?"

"No." Clara fought the urge to smooth down her dress, to touch her hair.

She straightened her shoulders and lifted her chin, the mantra that got her through the past year playing through her head on repeat.

Fake it till you make it.

Fake it till you make it.

"I'm the nanny."

CHAPTER TWO

"ABOUT THE NANNY mom hired for the girls." Brett stood beside Brody, his back to the fence, elbows hooked over the top. "How mad do you think Mom'll get if I go after her?"

"You're not fucking my daughters' nanny." Brody watched as the new nanny and his mom sat in the rockers on the wide porch of the main house, laughing and smiling like old friends.

"You say it like I don't plan on trying to do more than fuck her." Brett lifted one foot, hooking the heel of his boot over the bottom rail of the fence.

"I'm not sure you're cut out for chasing single mothers." Brody eyed his baby brother. "They'll chew you up and spit you out." He tipped his head to scan the front yard, looking for the little boy with hair the exact same dark shade as his momma. This place was busy, with ranch hands coming and going all day. The men were used to looking out for two tow-headed little girls, not quick-moving boys who didn't realize how dangerous a running horse could be.

"Might be worth it." Brett grinned. "You shoulda seen how pissed she was when she couldn't get in my truck."

"No one can get in that stupid thing. It needs running boards." Brody glanced back to where the woman sat on the porch, her legs crossed neatly at the ankles as she sipped the tea his mother always kept in the fridge. "She doesn't look like the kind to get pissed over much."

"I think looks might be deceiving on that one." Brett tipped his head to where the little boy ducked behind one of the work trucks. "I'm guessing it might have to do with the young ears that were around." His eyes came Brody's way. "You know how that goes."

"The girls are already ruined." Brody couldn't stop the smile his daughters always brought to his face. "Leah spilled her milk at breakfast and Mom got to hear the new word Wayne accidentally taught her."

"Poor Wayne." Brett glanced to where their mother sat. "She found him yet?"

"He's still breathing, so I'm guessing no." Brody kept his eye on the little boy as he followed behind one of the many barn cats wandering the property. "They done for the day on the back forty?"

"Not sure." Brett straightened off the fence. "Want me to go check before I take Clara back to get her car?"

Brody's attention dragged from where it had drifted. "Where's her car?"

"Ran it out of gas a couple miles down the road. It's packed full of her stuff. I'm guessing she'll want what's in it tonight."

"I'll take her." Brody's gaze eased Clara's way. "You go see if Wayne needs any help in the horse barn."

"So I can't chase her but you can?" Brett's tone was only half-joking.

Brody couldn't blame him. Clara was beautiful. More than.

Long dark hair. Wide eyes and full lips. She was not at all what he was expecting to end up with when his mother suggested bringing a nanny on staff.

That was the part he needed to remember. She was an employee of the ranch.

The ranch he ran.

"That's why you're not ready for the single mothers yet." Brody pushed off the fence and headed for the main house. "If you have to chase them you're doing it wrong." He kept walking as his brother scoffed.

That's what Brett didn't understand. Some women liked to be chased. Pursued doggedly.

Some didn't.

The key to success was knowing the difference between the two, and Clara definitely did not want to be chased.

Not that he'd be chasing her if she did.

His mother would kill him.

Brody stopped to watch Clara's little boy as he managed to get the feral barn cat to sniff his hand. "That's pretty impressive."

The little boy's head snapped Brody's way as he quickly pushed to his feet, staring up at Brody's face.

"She doesn't let anyone get near her." He tipped his head toward the cat lingering under the bumper of one of the trucks. "She usually runs away."

The little boy looked to the cat then back at Brody,

wariness in his dark eyes. "Brett said it was okay if I wanted to pet her."

"Wyatt." Clara hurried in between them, her eyes holding the same wariness as her son's as they met his. "If Mr. Pace doesn't want you to bother the cat then don't bother the cat." She wrapped one arm around Wyatt's shoulders, pulling him in tight.

Like she was protecting him.

"He wasn't bothering a thing." Brody moved back a half step, hoping to ease whatever concerns the new nanny had. "I think he was making a friend."

Clara's head tipped toward the cat, her eyes following a few seconds later.

The cat meowed their way as she rubbed against the closest truck's front tire.

"Brody Pace." His mother came down from the porch, pumping her arms as she hustled their way. "Stop bothering my new employee." She bumped past him, scooping up Clara and Wyatt as she went and hauling them back toward the house. "Brett said he would take you back to get your car." His mother paused, head turning as she scanned the yard for her youngest son.

"I'll take her."

His mother's face came Brody's way, brows lifting.

"Brett had something he had to do." Brody shoved one hand into the pocket of his jeans, fishing out the keys to his truck. "I've got time." He struggled not to focus on Clara. "And since it's my daughters she's watching we should probably get to know each other a little better."

His mother's eyes narrowed. "Hmph."

Clara's lips parted, her lower jaw dropping just a bit. "The twins are yours?"

He glanced his mother's way. It wasn't like her not to tell someone every bit of possible information there was to be had. "They are."

Clara eyed him a second longer, before finally tipping her head in a little nod. "That's fine then." She looked down the row of trucks always parked in front of the main house. "Your truck better not be ten feet off the ground." She stepped his way, turning when Wyatt stayed tucked into Maryann's side.

"It'll just be easier if he stays here with me." His mother waved one hand Clara's way. "We'll go find the girls so you can meet them when you get back."

"If you're sure it's okay." Clara glanced at Brody like he might be the one to have a problem with the situation.

"She's probably going to feed him cookies too." He turned toward his cherry red pickup. "Just so you know the full story."

Clara held one finger Wyatt's way. "Be a good guest."

"He's not a guest." Maryann pulled the little boy closer. "This is his home now."

Clara's eyes dropped to the ground. A heartbeat later she turned to follow Brody to the truck. He beat her there, opening the door and waiting.

Her sandals skidded to a stop as she rounded the bed, eyes meeting his. Her chin lifted a little as she started to walk again, barely pausing at the door he held open before hoisting herself into the passenger's seat. Brody closed the door, letting his hands rest on the frame of the open window. "I told you it was easier to get into."

Her gaze came his way for a second before snapping back to stare out the windshield. "Much easier."

Brody lingered for a second longer.

It'd been years since he'd had a woman besides his mother in his truck.

Three of them to be exact.

Clara peeked his way out of the corner of her eye.

"Okay." He backed away.

Thank God Brett wasn't around. He'd never let him live this down.

Brody climbed into the driver's seat and started the engine, slowly backing out, making triple sure no one was in his path before straightening out and heading down the long lane leading to the road running through their property.

"You said it's about two miles out?" He risked a glance Clara's way. Her head was angled toward the open window, eyes closed as the early summer air blew her hair from her face.

"Clara?"

She jumped a little, eyes flying open. "What?"

"Your car." He pointed down the road. "Brett said it was about two miles back toward town."

"Hopefully." She gave him a little smile before her full lips flattened out. "Unless it's been towed."

"No one's towing a car off Pace property, Darlin'." He gave her a grin. "There'd be hell to pay."

Her chin tucked a little. "It's not on your property. It's in the middle of the road."

Brody leaned back, relaxing a little in his seat. "All this is ours. Road included."

"Oh." Her head slowly turned back to stare out the front.

Everyone around here knew where Pace land started and ended. They were the largest property owner in the area. That alone carried enough weight no one would touch Clara's car.

Add in the Pace boys' reputation, and her car was as good as being under armed guard.

A small sedan came into view. Clara's shoulders eased down.

Brody pulled up alongside it before getting out and rounding the truck to open Clara's door. She gave him the same quizzical look she did when he opened the door earlier. Her eyes held his for a second before dropping as she slid from the seat. "Thank you."

"You wanna open the gas cover?" He went to the back end of his truck to retrieve the can he kept on hand.

Clara pressed the button on the fob, unlocking the doors before reaching in to click the tiny door open. "I didn't realize how far it was from the last gas station." The smooth skin of her cheeks barely flushed as she watched him pour the contents of the can into her empty tank.

"You're not the first. You won't be the last." He tipped out the last of the gasoline before twisting on the cap and pressing the cover back into place. "My momma runs hers out of gas at least twice a year."

Her eyes jumped to his. "Twice a year?"

He gave her a grin. "She's got a lot on her mind."

"It happens." Her lips barely lifted at the corners before settling back into the straight line that was beginning to bother him.

Not because she should smile more.

More because it seemed like maybe she didn't have enough to smile about.

Brody placed the can back in the open bed before tipping his head toward the road. "I'll follow you."

Clara nodded, tucking her long hair behind one ear as she turned to slide into her car. Once he heard her engine start Brody fired up his diesel, the sound immediately making it impossible to hear the sedan idling.

He waited while she buckled her belt and rolled down the windows.

After about a minute her brake lights flashed as she put it in drive and slowly took off, driving at a sensible speed down the road only he and his family and his men used.

For now.

She turned under the sign he had commissioned when his mother decided she wanted something to occupy her time, and fulfill a dream she'd had as long as he could remember.

Clara went slowly down the driveway, the lower set of her car resulting in the knock of gravel against metal as she went.

And her car didn't look like it could handle much more abuse.

Brody winced at every bang of rock against steel, guilt tugging at his gut for graveling the drive a month ago. The dirt under it was dusty and slippery when it rained, but it would have been a hell of a lot more gentle on her car.

Finally, Clara pulled into the spot at the very back of the line of cars, choosing it over a few closer to the house.

Brody honked his horn, his guilt worsening as she

jumped in her seat. When she turned his way he pointed to where she should be parking.

The men on the farm could walk.

Her eyes stayed on him in her side mirror.

He motioned with two fingers toward the front of the line of trucks.

It took more than a few heartbeats for her to finally put the car into reverse and back out of the spot. As she drove toward the house he whipped his truck into her vacated spot and shut down the engine, jumping out and heading straight for her car. She was just getting out when he made it to the trunk. "Pop your trunk and I'll help you unload."

Clara blinked. "To where?"

He pointed to the main house. "Right inside, Darlin." He lifted his pointer to the upper left window. "That one's yours."

She followed the path of his finger. "In the main house?"

Having a strange person so close seemed like a bad idea when his mother suggested it.

Now he was feeling a little different about the whole situation.

Brody stepped a little closer, chasing the soft scent the breeze kept stealing away. He moved the direction of his finger to the next window over. "That's my daughters' room."

Clara caught a bit of dark hair as it snagged on her lips, pulling it free of her mouth. "Do they get up much at night?"

Brody laughed. "Only to find their way into my bed."

Clara's eyes swept the front of the house. "Is your room far from theirs?"

He pointed to the third room in line. "It's right next door."

"Am I supposed to stop them from bothering you?"

Brody's arm dropped to his side. "They don't bother me." It was a little offensive that Clara thought she was brought in to keep him from having to play any role in his daughters' lives. "You're here so I can know they're safe while I work. At night they're my responsibility."

Her dark brows came together. "You're the one taking care of them at night?"

"Not sure why that's so hard for you to believe. They're my kids."

Clara's lips twisted into a flattened smile that held zero amusement. "That's an interesting perspective."

"It's not a perspective. It's the facts." Did she think he was an ass for needing help? For being unable to juggle full-time child care while running an entire goddamned ranch? "If you have a problem with the position you're filling, then you should probably tell me now."

Clara's dark brows lifted. "I'm not sure why you're getting so upset about this."

"I'm upset because you seem to think I'm some sort of negligent father who brought you in so he doesn't have to take care of his own damn kids."

"Aren't you?"

It looked like it was going to be a whole lot easier having Clara two doors down than he initially thought. Brody leaned in close as he passed her on his way to go find the two most important people in his life.

"No. I'm not."

CHAPTER THREE

THAT COULD HAVE gone better.

Clara stood in the middle of the drive, unsure where to go next for the second time since her arrival at Red Cedar Ranch.

So far today she'd managed to run her car out of gas and piss her new employer off.

If he was still her employer after that conversation.

The thought of having to pack Wyatt up and drive away from what she promised would be his new home made her stomach turn.

But so did working for a man who thought children were a burden he could push off on someone else.

Which apparently Brody was not.

It would have been a useful thing to consider before she went and made an ass out of herself for the second time today.

"Well, shit." Clara huffed out a breath. She needed this job, and right now there was a good chance it was no longer hers.

Time to nut up and apologize.

Clara marched along the path she'd just watched Brody take. At least five men passed her, each tipping their hat and drawling out a *ma'am* as she went by. She managed a smile for each of them, even though there was a very real possibility she might end up puking before she found Brody and tried to smooth this over.

And she had to smooth this over somehow.

The barn at the end of the worn path was huge. The outside was a deep red with a shining metal roof. A wide sliding door was partially open, giving her a peek into the space as she crept closer, trying to see if Brody was inside.

The scent of earth and animal filled the air as she leaned forward, attempting to get a better look. A horse whinnied loud and long as she carefully stepped through the door. Large fans hung from the rafters, the movement of the blades cooling the air more than she expected would be possible. Clara paused a few steps inside, listening for any sign Brody might be there.

A movement caught in her peripheral vision. She didn't have time to turn before something bumped into the side of her face, nudging her cheek.

She froze, turning her eyes as far as they would go toward the huge animal face less than an inch from her.

"Leave her alone, Edgar. She doesn't have anything for you."

Clara could barely breathe as the giant horse continued to bump into her.

"He won't hurt you." Brody ducked out of the stall a few doors down and came her way. "He's trying to sweet talk you into giving him something." He reached up to run one hand down the horse's snout, pushing his head away from hers.

Clara alternated looking between the beast and the man, trying to decide which one she should be more concerned about. One outweighed her by at least a thousand pounds, and the other held her and her son's future in his hands.

Fake it till you make it.

She swallowed down the fear she'd learned to live with over the past year, shoving it into the space she made for it, knowing it was there for the long haul. "I'm sorry."

Brody turned her way immediately, his long body and intense gaze making it impossibly clear who she should be most concerned about. "Are you?"

She almost winced at Brody's twist on the words she'd carelessly thrown at him. "I am."

He tipped his head in a nod that brought the brim of his hat over his eyes, hiding them from view.

Making it impossible to tell if he believed the truth she gave him.

She needed this job. Desperately.

Which meant she had to give him more of a reason to believe her apology was sincere.

"I, um…" She dropped her eyes to the dusty ground between them. It wasn't easy to admit her ex-husband's failings, especially since they were her failings too.

She failed to see him for what he was.

Failed to do anything about it when she did.

Brody held one hand up. "It's fine." He turned to walk away, sending the ever-present panic climbing up her throat.

"It's not." The words jumped out, filling the quiet barn with more force than she intended. "It's not." She said it softer, trying to be the calm, collected person she needed to be. Letting her frustration at literally everything bleed into this conversation would only hurt her more. "I'm not used to men who are okay helping take care of their children."

It was a dramatic understatement, but it got the point across.

Brody's wide body slowly turned her way. "Okay with helping?" He snorted out an unamused chuckle. "I enjoy my daughters." He came a step closer, his boots scuffing against the ground as he did. His jaw went tight. "I'm not sure what kind of men you're used to dealing with, but if they think their kids are a burden then you should probably find a way to get rid of them quick."

"I did." The admission was quiet and only partially correct.

She hadn't gotten rid of Richard. He'd technically rid himself of her.

And ten years wasn't quick.

But gone was gone, right?

Brody's blue eyes rested on her face, the shadow of his hat making them seem darker than they did in the light. "Hold out your hand."

It was an odd request, but at this point she'd do anything to keep this job. Clara held her hand out, prepared to shake on their truce.

Brody's fingers brushed hers, rough and well-used as they gently turned her palm up. He rested an oblong reddish ball about the size of a cherry tomato in her hand. "Give that to Edgar. He'll be your best friend forever."

She turned to the chocolate brown horse watching her with long-lashed eyes. "Do I just stick it in his mouth?"

"With Edgar you can do it pretty much however." Brody came a little closer, an odd smell coming along with him.

It was a little like leather. A little like the earthy smell of the barn.

And man. He smelled very much like a man. One who worked a job that made his hands rough and his skin sweat.

"The best thing you can do is hold your hand almost flat." He settled his hand under hers, the wide expanse of his palm resting against her knuckles. "Curve it just enough so he doesn't accidentally knock the treat loose." Brody moved her hand under Edgar's searching lips, holding it steady as they tickled their way across her fingers in search of the snack she offered. His teeth crunched into the hard snack as his lips continued to search for more. Once he made absolutely sure that was all she had, Edgar's nose came to bump her face again.

"Greedy." Brody pushed at the horse's head. "She doesn't want to pet you."

"He wants me to pet him?" She had zero experience with horses and sort of assumed they weren't very interested in affection.

"He wants whatever you'll give him." Brody stroked down the horse's neck, smoothing along Edgar's shining coat.

Clara lifted her hand, pulling it back as Edgar's nose immediately came for it.

"He's just checking you out." Brody flattened his hand against Edgar's cheek. "Gotta be patient, buddy. Let her come to you."

Clara peeked Brody's way as she attempted to mimic his

hand placement. Edgar huffed out a breath as she rested her hand against his face. "Good boy."

If someone told her a year ago she'd be standing in a barn petting a horse she would have laughed. The thought was crazy.

As crazy as the path that led her here.

"Daddy." The high-pitched squeal of a tiny voice pierced the first quiet moment she'd had in forever.

Clara turned as a curly-haired little girl sprinted toward Brody, her arms held high over her head. "I can see Egger?"

"Of course you can see Edgar." Brody caught her as she leapt at him, swinging her little body high in the air before tucking her against his chest. "Did you bring him a snack?"

The little girl's eyes went as wide as her smile as she dug into the pocket of her chambray shorts, coming out with a baby carrot clutched in her chubby hand. "I has a carrot."

Brody twisted her toward Edgar. The horse slowly and carefully worked the carrot free, his flapping lips sending the little girl into a fit of giggles. She clapped her hands, still grinning from ear to ear. "He bite me."

"He didn't bite you." Brody pinched at her belly. "Silly Monster."

The little girl suddenly seemed to notice she and her daddy weren't alone, the blue eyes that perfectly matched her daddy's coming Clara's way. "Who's that?"

"That is Miss—"

"Clara. My name is Clara." She smiled, barely managing to get the expression on her lips before Edgar bumped her again, this time surprising her enough to make her laugh.

Brody's daughter laughed along with her, the wide smile

she'd had since coming into the barn proving to be a little contagious. "Eggar's funny."

"He is, isn't he?" Clara turned to the horse, reaching out to give the white patch between his eyes a little pat.

"Leah?" Maryann ducked into the barn, her shoulders dropping as she caught sight of the little girl tucked into her daddy's arms. "What have I told you about coming out to the barn alone?"

Leah turned to Clara. "S'not safe."

Clara nodded her head. "That's right." It'd been a while since she'd dealt with a three-year-old, and it was nice to know she still understood the vernacular. "Gotta take a grown-up with you."

Leah turned to Brody. "Daddy's grown up."

"That's debatable." Maryann let out a breath. "It's almost supper time. Get in the house and get washed up."

"Yes, ma'am." Brody set Leah on her feet. The little girl immediately took off, racing out of the barn and along the grass toward the house.

"You too." Maryann waved them along, her eyes meeting Clara's. "Wyatt's almost got the table set."

Clara blinked a few times, trying to control the emotion threatening to rear its ugly head. She gave Maryann a nod before turning to Edgar, using the horse as an excuse to take a second.

He tucked his face alongside hers, almost seeming to rest his head on her shoulder as she smoothed down his neck the same way she'd seen Brody do a few minutes earlier. She took a few deep breaths before backing away, offering him one last pat on the cheek before turning to Maryann, a smile firmly in place. "What can I do to help?"

Maryann smiled wide. "Don't get me started on that." She reached out to wrap one arm around Clara's shoulders. "There's never a shortage of things to be done around here." She led her from the barn, leaving Brody standing with Edgar as she continued to chatter about all there was to be juggled.

Clara peeked behind them.

Just a quick look. Only to see if Brody was coming with them.

But he still stood in the same spot she left him, eyes holding hers.

"Do you like pork roast?"

Clara snapped her attention to Maryann. "Doesn't everyone?"

Maryann's smile brightened. "I knew I liked you." She gave Clara's shoulders a squeeze. "Remind me to mail Cliff a thank you note for sending you my way."

"How do you know Cliff?" Her attorney never fully explained how he came to know Maryann or why he wanted to help her find a nanny from states away.

Maryann glanced around. "You can't tell anyone." She leaned in closer, the skin of her cheeks pinking just a little. "He and I dated in college."

Clara eyed the woman at her side. Brody's mother was beautiful. Trim and warm with smooth skin and light brown hair that fell in soft sweeps to her chin. "You dated Cliff?"

"College was a long time ago." She lifted her shoulders in a little shrug. "And he was certainly better looking back then." Her perfectly arched brows lifted. "And studying to be an attorney, so there was that."

"But you didn't stay with him."

Maryann's lips eased into a soft smile. "No. I did not."

Her gaze lifted to where a line of men made their way across the yard. "And I've never regretted it for a single second."

Maryann might not, but Clara would bet her ass Cliff kicked himself every morning and night over letting her slip away.

Clara watched as Brody fell in line with the other four men walking toward the house. She recognized one of them as Brett, but a striking resemblance meant the others were simple enough to guess. "Those are your sons."

"All four of 'em and their daddy." Maryann shook her head. "I swear the man couldn't make a girl if he tried."

"They are more complicated to produce."

Maryann's head turned her way. "Hell yes they are." She squeezed Clara again. "Have I told you how glad I am that you're here?"

She had. At least ten times already.

"I'm glad I'm here too." Clara felt lost for so long.

And somehow in less than a day Maryann made her feel like there was finally a place for her in the world.

One she found all on her own.

"Look at that pretty thing." The man in the middle headed straight their way, his blue eyes locked on Maryann. "You get your hair done today?" He caught her in his arms, spinning her into a little dance as he scooted them across the porch. Maryann's head fell back as she laughed, leaning away like she knew the arms around her would hold tight.

Like she knew he had her.

And he did. The man spun her once before Maryann managed to wiggle away enough to turn to Clara. "Clara, this is Bill." She elbowed him as he tried to grab her again. "I wish I could say he's normally better behaved than this."

Bill's smile held as he reached one hand Clara's way. "You're the new Monster wrangler."

Clara took his hand in the strong shake she'd practiced a million times, her eyes finding Brody. "Yes?"

Two giggly roars carried through the screen door just as a set of blondes hit the center brace, knocking it open, roars continuing as they rushed their grandpa. Bill immediately stumbled back, pretending to suffer under their ambush a second before grabbing them both, scooping one up under each arm and walking toward the door Maryann held open. He leaned in to press a kiss to her lips as he passed.

The two brothers she hadn't met yet paused to introduce themselves as they passed into the house. Boone and Brooks were both definitely younger than Brody, but besides that she couldn't begin to guess the order of the brothers.

"You get your car okay?" Brett lingered where she stood.

"I did." She glanced to where it was parked, still packed with what few things she and Wyatt had left after selling the second-hand furniture she'd accrued after moving out of Richard's house. "It was still right where we left it."

"Knew it would be." Brett smiled. "I'd be happy to help you unpack that after supper."

CHAPTER FOUR

HE MIGHT HAVE to string Brett up by his boots.

Clara's dark eyes moved from Brett to Brody before moving back to the youngest Pace brother. "That's kind of you to offer, but I'll be fine."

"Boys." Their mother's sharp tone cut its way through the screen door. "Let the girl come in and eat." She pushed the door open, coming out to pull Clara into the house. "She's had a long day."

Brody waited until his mother was out of earshot before turning to his brother. "Back off."

Brett's eyes widened in false innocence. "I can't even be nice to her?"

Brody pushed past his brother, bumping him with his shoulder as he went. "Nope."

He went into the house he'd only lived outside of a few short years. His mother and Clara stood in the kitchen, Maryann Pace passing out filled dishes as Clara helped the girls wash their hands in the wide sink. The girls never knew a stranger. A fact that became very clear when Michaela latched onto Clara as she tried to ease the little girl's feet to the floor.

Clara tipped a little, the unexpected dangling of the toddler only throwing her off for a second before she bounced Michaela's little body onto her hip.

Leah stared up at where her sister was, lifting her arms above her head. "I want up too."

Brody took a step closer, intending to scoop his free daughter up and save Clara from the situation. But before he could, Clara crouched down and hefted Leah up, balancing her on the other hip, laughing as the girls giggled. It was the first easy smile he'd seen on Clara's lips.

"Are you hungry?" Clara made her way into the dining area where his mother was shifting around chairs and barking out orders at his brothers. Wyatt stood off to one side, looking a little overwhelmed, his hands clutching the back of the chair in front of him.

Brody worked his way to the little boy's side. "That where you want to sit?"

Wyatt's eyes went to Maryann. "This is where Miss Maryann told me to go."

"Then it sounds like your seat's right next to mine." Brody pulled out the chair next to the one Wyatt gripped tight. "Did you get washed up?"

Wyatt tipped his head in a nod as he continued to watch the movements of the people around him.

"Then maybe you can save my seat while I go hit the sink myself."

Wyatt's eyes finally came his way. "Okay."

Brody gave him a smile. "Thanks." He glanced Clara's way, making sure she was okay with the girls before going to the sink and scrubbing away the dust and dirt he'd collected since lunch. By the time he was back Wyatt was sitting in his seat as Maryann scooped his plate full of food. One of the little boy's arms stretched across to rest in the seat of the next chair over.

Wyatt pointed to the vacant spot. "No one tried to take it."

"That's cause they didn't want to mess with you." Brody eased down into the seat and came face to face with Clara. She sat right across from him, a little blonde girl on each side. Her eyes caught his for a second as she helped Leah avoid flipping an entire scoop of mashed potatoes across the table.

A bowl hit him in the center of the chest. "Here."

Brody lifted his attention to his frowning mother as he took the dish of rolls. "Thank you."

"Um-hm." Her narrowed eyes held his for a second longer before she turned back to Wyatt, her expression softening immediately. "What about the pork roast honey? How much of that do you want?"

Wyatt's eyes went to Clara. "Just a little, I think."

"Now that doesn't sound right for a growing boy." Maryann pointed at Brody before her finger moved to where his brothers sat. "Do you think my boys got as big as they are just eating a little bit of anything?"

Wyatt looked around the table. "No?"

"Darn right." Maryann dropped a chunk of meat on Wyatt's plate. "You want gravy on all of it?"

Wyatt blinked. "Yes?"

"Good boy. Gravy makes everything better." His mother poured a thick stream of gravy over Wyatt's potatoes and meat before shoving the boat Brody's way without even looking. "If you eat all that you can have seconds." She patted Wyatt's shoulder on her way to the seat at one end of the table.

It was strange not having the girls at his side. They'd owned the spots since they were big enough to sit, starting in high chairs before moving on to the booster seats they currently occupied.

But it was clear he wasn't the only one experiencing something different at the dinner table. Wyatt sat silently, watching the men at the table laugh as they ate and talked about the events of the day. The kid looked like he was watching aliens land in the front yard.

"What kind of stuff do you like to do, Wyatt?" Brody hoped to distract the boy from the loud chaos that was his brothers. Clara seemed to be on the quiet side, and that probably meant poor Wyatt was overwhelmed.

Wyatt turned Brody's way, a bit of roll peeking through his lips. "I dunno."

"You don't know what you like to do for fun?" He thought maybe Wyatt was still struggling with all that'd been thrown his way today.

Wyatt shook his head. "Not now. I use-ta like to play video games but we couldn't take the player with us when we left."

What Brody hoped would be a lighthearted conversation about swimming or bike riding took a hard left, dragging him deep into waters a man should be able to wade his way through. "I see."

"My dad said it was his so we couldn't take it." Wyatt

grabbed his fork and dug into the food on his plate, seemingly unbothered by the nature of the conversation.

Probably because it was the life he was used to.

Brody glanced around the table full of people who would always have his back no matter what. His father and mother and brothers were the people he knew would be at his side no matter what went down, and the fact that anything like that was foreign to this little boy stuck him deep in the gut.

"I'm all done." Michaela shoved her way back from the table and the plate of barely-touched food in front of her. Brody started to stand, ready to chase his daughter down and wrangle her back to her seat.

Clara immediately pushed the chair back in place. "Gotta eat your broccoli so your brain grows big." Clara stabbed the pink plastic fork beside Michaela's plate into a broccoli spear and held it up. "If you want to be the queen of the world you will need a big brain."

Michaela shook her head. "Not the queen." She grabbed the fork and shoved the vegetable into her mouth. "I be the king."

Clara's mouth softened to a little smile. "Smart girl."

Michaela grinned around her broccoli. "Yeah."

"I be the king too." Leah shoved a chunk of her own broccoli in with her fingers. "We will bofe be the king."

Clara managed to get both girls to clean their plates before magically talking them into clearing their own places. By the time both spots were empty, Brody managed to wolf down his food in time to snag the girls and take them upstairs, leaving Clara and Wyatt in the kitchen with his family.

Not that he didn't want to be around them, but right now

he needed a little space to wrap his head around the situation.

What kind of man would keep something his child enjoyed?

Maybe man was the wrong word.

Brody took the girls into the bathroom attached to his bedroom and filled the tub, scrubbing both girls down and washing their hair before lining them up in front of the sink to brush their teeth. Morning came early on the ranch, and the earlier he got them to sleep the earlier he could get to sleep.

Once their hair was combed he tucked them into the toddler beds they'd moved into about a year ago, set the slowly spinning star projector to play them to sleep, and crept out, silently backing from the room.

"Oop." Clara jumped back as he nearly bumped into her. "Sorry. I was just—"

"Nothing to apologize for." He'd been prepared to feel a little odd about having someone he didn't know in the house. Even after his mother assured him she'd found a perfect fit, Brody still expected it to be strange.

Intrusive.

But nothing about Clara seemed to be intrusive.

"Are you ready to unload your car?"

"I can get it." She held up the box in her hand like it would make him agree she should have to unload it all by herself. "I was taking this to the office for your mother. It was in the room where Wyatt's staying."

Brody glanced down at the box that turned out to be full of his mother's things. He reached out to gently pry it from

Clara's grip. "I'll get this and then we can go get what's in your car."

"It's really not a big deal." She started to back away. "I can get it. Thanks though." She gave him a tight smile as she backed around the corner leading to the stairs.

If Wyatt's father was the kind of man who kept a game his son wanted then he was probably the kind of man who didn't treat a woman the way she deserved to be treated either. The thought aggravated the hell out of him.

Brody quickly dropped the box off in his mother's office before going down the stairs in search of Clara. She was digging in the backseat of her car when he found her, pulling out a box that she could barely get her arms around. "Let me get this." Brody stepped in, taking it from her. He peeked in the top at the contents. Neat piles of clothing filled the container, but it was impossible to tell who the items belonged to. "Is this going to your room or Wyatt's?"

Her chin lifted just a little. "Either is fine."

Clara might seem all sweet and quiet, but the woman had a stubborn streak that might be wider than he first realized. "Okay." Brody hoofed it back up the stairs, setting the box on the floor near the closet in Clara's room before turning to go retrieve more. She ducked past him with a box in her arms, setting it on the bed before walking by him and going back down the stairs. He followed after her. A few plastic boxes with toiletries were in the floorboards. Clara leaned in to collect them as Brody popped the trunk and went to start unloading what was in there.

He stood at the open lid, staring in at the contents.

Pillows and blankets were stacked inside, along with a few smaller boxes. "Are you having the rest delivered?"

Clara bumped the back door closed. "There is no more." She turned away, walking quickly toward the house, leaving him standing in the cooling night air.

There wasn't a single toy in the car. Not one thing that wouldn't be considered a necessity.

He glanced up at the woman who held more secrets than he realized, watching as she went up the steps to the porch.

No wonder Clara questioned his willingness to take care of his daughters.

His dedication to their happiness.

Brody grabbed the contents of the trunk, managing to get everything in one armload. He stomped his way up the stairs, each step pissing him off more.

He couldn't help the heavy hit of his boots against the wood floor of her bedroom as he went in. Clara stood in the corner, eyes far from him. "You can put it on the bed."

He laid the pile down, being careful not to tip out the boxes he had stacked on the pillows, then turned to face her.

Her gaze refused to meet his. "Thank you for your help."

He opened his mouth, ready to ask about shit that was none of his business.

"Mom." Wyatt stepped into the room, his head immediately coming Brody's way. "Oh. Hey, Mr. Pace."

"Brody." He dipped his head. "You can call me Brody."

He didn't want this kid to feel like he was someone he had to tiptoe around. Especially now.

Wyatt looked to his mother.

"If Mr. Pace wants you to call him Brody, then that's what you should do."

Brody worked his jaw at Clara's words. "I would prefer you call me Brody too."

She ignored him, her attention overly focused on her son. "Give me just a minute and I'll be ready to read your story."

Wyatt clutched a worn paperback in his hands. The edges were frayed and split and the colors were faded. "Okay." He lifted one hand in a little wave. "Goodnight, Mr. —" He almost smiled. "Brody."

"Goodnight, Wyatt."

As soon as Wyatt was out of earshot he turned back Clara's way. "I—"

She finally lifted her eyes to his. "Thank you for your help. I need to get Wyatt ready for bed."

He pressed his lips together.

Pride was something he understood well.

The few items he'd carried in didn't even come close to filling the closet or drawers in Clara's room. Her desire to unload them on her own was most likely to keep him from knowing her situation.

And he'd taken that from her.

"Goodnight, Clara."

She took a little breath, her shoulders lining up as she did. "Goodnight, Brody."

He forced his feet out of her room and down the hall to his. Even after he was shaved, showered, and dressed in the t-shirt and shorts he always slept in, the thought of Wyatt's dad keeping that damn game still bothered him.

He couldn't imagine not letting his daughters have anything he owned if it brought them joy. They were what got him through the shock of their mother's death, and the thought of keeping any happiness they could have made him edgy.

Irritated.

Brody didn't even try to lay down. It was already clear sleep was a long way off for him, so he took the back stairs of the large farmhouse, heading down to the kitchen. He dug through the fridge, pulling out a pack of pre-sliced cheddar cheese and a bottle of water before grabbing a pack of crackers and heading out to the screened-in back porch.

He caught the screen door as it started to whip closed, making sure it softly slid into place before going toward the line of gliding rockers that faced the open fields.

He stopped short, bare feet scuffing against the smooth wood planks.

The porch wasn't as empty as he expected it to be.

CHAPTER FIVE

WELL SHIT.

Clara thought everyone in the house was asleep. Expected she could finally have a minute alone to process the events of the day.

Hell, maybe even the events of her freaking mess of a life.

"I'm sorry." Clara stood, ready to escape the man who always seemed to find her at the most inconvenient of times. "I was just—"

"There's nothing to be sorry for." Brody came closer, holding out the bottle of water in his hand. "Thirsty?"

She eyed it. She was most definitely thirsty, but digging through the family fridge and cabinets felt invasive.

"Take it." He set it on the table next to the chair she'd just jumped out of. "There's always some in the house and a bunch in the fridge out here." He went to the refrigerator tucked into the corner of the enclosed porch, opening the door wide. The glow of the interior light filled the space as Brody grabbed one of what must have been a hundred bottles of water before letting the door swing back into place. "We keep 'em out here for the ranch hands. That way they don't have to try to get their boots clean to come into the house whenever they're thirsty."

She'd assumed it would be as odd for them as it was for her to be here, sharing space with someone she didn't really know. It hadn't occurred to her there would be many other people like her here. "Do you have many ranch hands?"

"Define many." Brody cracked the lid on his water as he eased down into the chair right next to the one she'd occupied for the past fifteen minutes. "Right now we're in the process of expanding, so we're trying to find about ten more, which will bring us to about thirty."

Wow.

Clara slowly lowered back into the chair, trying to come to terms with the vastness of her new employer's operation. "You said the road leading here was part of the property." Clara turned to look out over the darkened landscape. "How big is it here?"

"Well over twenty thousand acres." Brody's tone was casual. Like they were discussing something as mundane as the weather.

She turned to look out the side of the porch. "How far does that go?"

"If you can see it, it's Pace land." He worked the end of the sleeve of crackers he brought out with him open, dropping a piece of cheese onto one before holding it out her way.

She was about to reject his offer when Brody pushed it closer. "Take it. I know you didn't get much eating done with the girls tonight."

"They were very good at dinner." She finally caved in and

took the snack, biting off half as Brody popped an entire cheese cracker in his own mouth.

"Doesn't mean they gave you time to eat." He leaned back in his chair, stretching his long legs out as he began to slowly glide back and forth.

She dared a peek at his bare feet and the legs attached to them. It was already strange seeing him in something besides boots and jeans.

And that damn hat.

Never in her life would she have imagined what a cowboy hat could do for a man. It was the equivalent of heels on a woman. Taking a perfectly fine looking man and transforming him into something much more dangerous in an instant.

And Brody Pace was definitely dangerous. It was written all over him.

From the easy way he moved, to the slow drawl of his words. The man was all kinds of trouble wrapped up in a package so pretty it pissed her off.

And then he put a damn hat on it.

Maryann could have at least prepared her for the situation. Let her in on the secret that the father of the twins she was hired to care for was a certified cowboy.

A widowed cowboy.

"Can I ask you something?" She'd been trying to get the information out of Maryann all day, but the fate of Brody's wife was the one thing his mother decided to be tight-lipped on.

"If I can ask you something."

It was a pretty decent deal, especially considering Brody was probably going to ask her something related to her experience caring for kids. "I think you might be getting the bum end of that deal."

"I doubt it." Brody's gaze changed. Even in the dark it was easy to see. The intensity it held was different from what she'd seen from him all evening. "You want to know what happened to my wife." Brody held out another cheese cracker. "And I want to know what happened to Wyatt's father."

Her spine went stiff at the mention of the bastard who ruined not just hers, but also Wyatt's life in the blink of an eye. "Does it matter what happened?"

"Seems like it does." Brody popped another cracker stack into his mouth, continuing that slow rock as he watched her.

Waiting to see what she'd give him.

Honestly his guess was as good as hers at this point.

Clara rested her hands in her lap, holding the cracker as she looked out over the moonlit night.

Maybe Richard hadn't ruined her life as much as she thought he had.

"His name is Richard."

"Dick. Got it." Brody tipped back his water, draining half. "Continue."

"He goes by Richard."

"Course he does." Brody leaned her way. "But it's not the name he deserves, is it?"

She couldn't disagree. "He's an ass."

"That's what I gathered."

"You gathered?" She'd done her best to keep what happened from Maryann. It didn't matter and she was so flipping tired of people looking at her with pity in their eyes.

"Wyatt said he liked to play games, but Dick wouldn't let him take them when you left."

Clara slid the cracker in her hand onto the table between them as her stomach clenched tight. "There was a lot he wouldn't let us take when we left."

It was something she did her best to make light of with Wyatt. She tried to make him feel like they had what really mattered. Promised him that everything they left behind would be replaced.

And she planned to make good on the offer.

"Where is he now?" The edge in Brody's question sent a ripple down her spine.

Not of fear, even though there was a definite feeling that maybe Richard should hope to never run into the man at her side.

"Still in California. With his pregnant girlfriend."

"He's having another kid?" Brody tapped one bare foot against the wood planks running the length of the porch. "What a dick."

"Pretty much." The air left her lungs a little easier than it had in a while. "He's an awful human."

"He's a dick." Brody's head turned from side to side. "You can say it now. There's no little ears around."

"He is a dick."

Brody picked up the cracker she discarded and held it back out. "So you want to know about my wife."

Clara took the cheese cracker again. "I just thought it might be useful since I'm taking care of her daughters."

Brody's gaze held hers for a few long seconds. "She never knew them."

The thought brought a lump to her throat. Having Wyatt

was the single best thing that had ever happened to her. Without him she would have been lost this past year. She would have had no reason to fight like she had. "That doesn't mean they're not still hers."

Brody's eyes finally moved away to stare straight ahead, out toward the open field behind the house. "I think for a long time it was too hard for me to think of them as hers. She wanted them so much, and knowing she never even got to touch them was—" He cleared his throat.

"She didn't know them." Clara played with the hem of the dress she'd been wearing for almost twenty hours. "But do they know *her*?"

Brody's head dipped in a little nod. "As much as they can."

It was easy enough to read between the lines and figure out his wife died bringing her daughters into the world. "Maybe you can tell me more about her sometime."

He was silent for a long time. Long enough Clara thought maybe she'd pushed too far asking to know more about the woman he clearly loved very much.

"The girls look just like her."

"She was beautiful then."

Brody glanced her way. "She was." He chuckled low. "A terrible cook though."

"Cooking's overrated." Clara could almost imagine Brody trying to choke down something completely inedible and pretending it was the best thing he'd ever eaten.

"Not when you're hungry." He laughed a little. "But she could sing like nothing I've ever heard."

"Well that makes up for the cooking then." Clara relaxed back in her chair, letting her head rest against the tall back of the seat as she started to rock it. "I can't sing and I would only call my cooking tolerable at best."

"But you're a hell of a mom and that makes up for anything else."

"How do you know what kind of mother I am?"

Brody's head turned her way, his eyes once again coming to hers in a way that made her want to shift in her seat. "Because I've met your son, and it sounds like Dick didn't have shit to do with the way Wyatt turned out."

———

"CLA-LA?" LEAH STOOD in the door to Clara's room, her curly hair still damp from the bath Brody gave her before tucking her into bed.

The same bed she promptly snuck out of, just like she had the last four nights.

Clara flipped back the covers on the queen-sized bed in the room where she was staying. "Hurry up. Wyatt will be here in just a minute."

Leah's bare feet slapped against the floor and she ran across the room to climb up and into the bed.

"Where's Mich—"

"I coming too." Michaela's little voice carried into the room along with her own racing steps as she sprinted down the hall.

Michaela and Leah settled under the covers, wiggling down against the pillows as they got comfortable. Clara scooted in next to them, leaving her other side free for Wyatt.

Her son peeked into the room, his sweet face breaking into a smile when he saw the twins were already there.

She worried at first he might not appreciate the girls moving in on the time she'd given to only him since the day he was born. From day one she'd cuddled with him and read the same story before bed. A book she'd read as a child, wishing there was someone to read it to her.

Someone to read anything to her.

Wyatt climbed into the bed, taking up the remaining space as he passed the book to Clara. After eight years of nightly reads it was worn and practically falling apart, but Wyatt refused to let her read anything else.

She tipped her head toward the twins. "You ready?"

The girls' heads bobbed as their little toes wiggled around under the blankets.

"What's going on in here?"

She knew it was only a matter of time before Brody discovered their clandestine story time, and honestly she was a little surprised at how long it took him. "Story time."

Brody lifted a brow. "I think you need a bigger bed if you're going to hold nightly book reading events."

Michaela's head snapped Clara's way. "Daddy's bed is big."

"I don't think—"

The twins were already up and moving. After almost a week on the ranch, she knew exactly why Maryann decided to bring on an extra set of hands to keep an eye on the girls.

Because they went a hundred miles an hour from the time their feet hit the floor until the time their heads hit the pillow.

And then some.

"Come on Wy-it." Leah grabbed his hand as she went,

pulling as hard as she could. Michaela joined in, the girls doing a pretty decent job of pulling a hesitant Wyatt along.

Brody took a step back as the clog of kids moved into the hallway. He watched after them, hands on his jean-clad hips.

Clara climbed out of the bed and held the book Brody's way. "You'll need this."

He shook his head. "Not a story reader." He tipped his head toward where his room was located. "You can read to them. I'm going to go downstairs."

She glanced toward his room.

"Take your time." Brody headed toward the front stairs. "I have a few things I need to take care of."

Clara stood in the empty hall a second longer, tapping one foot against the floor. She'd done her best to stay away from Brody as much as possible since their night on the porch, trying to put some distance between them. It's what she should have done from the very beginning.

And now somehow she was about to end up in his bed.

Not in any sort of interesting way.

Which she definitely had not already thought about.

"Cla-la." Michaela's holler was a little too loud.

"I'm coming."

The kids were all lined up along the wide, king-sized mattress when she made it to the doorway. She hadn't peeked into this room for the same reason she'd done her best to avoid any more situations where she and Brody would be alone.

He was her employer. She needed this job. Worked hard to get it.

That meant the lines between them had to be thick and wide.

Clara perched on the edge of the bed, refusing to look around like she wanted to. She flipped open the book and started flying through the pages. It was the fastest she'd ever read the story as she rushed through, racing against whatever Brody was off doing.

Even at the accelerated pace, both girls were asleep by the time she was finished and Wyatt's eyes were glazed. Clara closed the book and patted Wyatt's leg. "Come on. Let's get these girls to their beds."

"You can leave them."

The sound of Brody's voice was soft and smooth.

And different.

It sent her to her feet and spinning toward the open doorway. "I thought you said you had things to do."

"I did." His eyes held hers. "And you're an awful fast reader."

"I was trying to be considerate." Clara crossed her arms over the t-shirt she wore. Her pajamas were what many people would wear in public, but being in Brody's bedroom in them still carried a level of intimacy she was trying desperately to avoid creating between them.

He stepped into the room, bringing the comfortable discomfort she had with the situation to a completely different level. "Are you sure you weren't trying to avoid me?"

Of freaking course she was trying to avoid him.

The man was problematic from his hat-smashed hair to his boot-clad toes and all the tight t-shirts and worn jeans in between. He was everything a smart woman would try to corral into being hers.

Not that she'd been a smart woman, historically speaking.

But Brody didn't seem to understand the parameters of their situation, and that was just as problematic as everything else about him. Clara turned to where her son was staring at the ceiling, his lids dropping in slow, languid blinks. "Wyatt honey, it's time to go to your bed."

He turned her way, eyes wide as he fought to hold them open. "Uh-kay."

She watched as her son passed the man making her feel less sane with each passing day. "Night, Brody."

"Good night, Little Man." Brody's soft smile at her son cut straight to her heart.

And it pissed her off.

"Stop it." She snapped it out, creeping close enough she was sure Brody would be the only one to hear her hushed words.

"Stop what?" The man had the audacity to act innocent. Like he had no idea how difficult he could make her life.

Which only made her more angry. "You know exactly what I'm talking about." Clara pointed at his chest, catching herself just before stabbing the tip of her finger into what would certainly be a wall of pure muscle. "You are my boss. I cannot be in your room in my pajamas."

Brody's eyes dropped between them, moving down the baggy t-shirt and banded-ankle sweats she wore. "Those are your pajamas?"

"What?" Clara looked down at the shirt she bought at the very first concert she went to as an eighteen-year-old college student. Right before Richard showed up and changed the trajectory of her whole life. "Of course these are my—" Her eyes snapped back to his. "Stop distracting me."

"You find me distracting?"

Her brain stumbled. "That's not what I said."

"That's almost exactly what you said." Brody eased a little closer, bringing his chest to her still pointing finger, proving it was just as solid as she expected. "And I think you're confused about your position here at the ranch." He leaned down, bringing that rugged scent of outdoors and working man along with him. "Because I'm not your boss, Darlin'."

CHAPTER SIX

BRODY PEEKED INTO his daughters' room as he passed by their door. Both beds were empty.

The house was quiet. Much too quiet for the Little Monsters to be awake.

He walked toward the stairs, being careful not to let his work boots bang against the wood boards. Clara's door was cracked as he passed, and the movement of light through the opening caught his eye. A familiar pattern spun across the ceiling of the still-dark room.

A pile of blond curls stuck out from under the blankets and a chubby leg was flung across the pillow next to it.

That explained why they'd stopped climbing into his bed.

Brody pulled the door closed to keep Clara and the girls from being disturbed. Looked like he'd have to come up with a way to stop them from bothering Clara. She cared for them all day while he worked, he didn't expect her to take the night shift too.

He took the stairs in quick steps, trying to push the thought of Clara and his girls tucked into bed together to the back of his mind.

His mother was downstairs finishing up the breakfast she put together every morning for him and any hands that wanted to partake.

Most of them usually did considering it meant they didn't have to fend for themselves.

Brody paused on his way out the back door to grab a piece of bacon from the large platter sitting on the counter. "I'm going to go check on Penny. See how she's feeling this morning." They had a pregnant mare that was beginning to show signs she would be foaling soon and he wanted to keep a close eye on her.

It was what brought him to the barn the night before.

And what led to Clara being on his bed, ruining all his chances for a good night's sleep.

The air was cool but humid as he crossed the yard toward the barn they used to house foaling mares and the family horses. The soft sound of cooing made him pause just outside the door.

"I think this is your favorite, isn't it?" Clara's words were light. Relaxed. Nothing like what he was used to hearing come out of her mouth.

Brody cleared his throat, giving her a second of warning before he pulled the slider open.

She and Edgar both stared at him.

He tipped his head Clara's way. "Morning."

The woman who occupied more of his thoughts with each passing day held a chunk of apple in her barely-curved palm just like he'd showed her, staring him down as Edgar searched for it across her hand.

"You don't have to sneak out here to feed him." Brody moved closer to where she stood, craving the nearness they'd shared her first night on the ranch.

"I'm not sneaking." She turned to Edgar, reaching up to scratch his cheek. "I just like coming out here when it's quiet." Her eyes came to him. "So I can be alone."

"Got a mare about to have her foal in this barn, Darlin'. Probably not the best place to go to be alone." Brody leaned against the side of Edgar's stall. "Best way to be alone here is to ride Edgar out to one of the resting pastures."

He'd been trying to find a way to get Clara alone since their night on the porch, but she was clearly hell-bent on making it as difficult as possible.

Not that he blamed her. Clara came from a very different world than he had. Seemed like she expected to be booted off the ranch for one wrong move.

She clearly didn't realize the way things worked in the Pace household.

"I'll keep that in mind." She tried to move away from Edgar's stall, but Brody stepped right in her path.

"You ever ridden a horse?" He knew the answer. Was banking on it. Planned to use it and her clear affection for his mother's horse to his advantage.

She glanced toward Edgar, but her lips remained sealed together.

"What if I take you out today?" He was set to make a round of the east side of the property today. Check to see which pastures were ready for rotation and which still needed more time. "Show you the ranch."

Clara's brows came together. "What about the girls?"

"It's Saturday." Brody tipped the rim of his hat back a little. "That's the day my mom and dad take them into town for lunch and ice cream."

She didn't immediately reject the idea, which meant he was closer to having her to himself than he'd managed to get in almost a week.

It had been years since he'd felt this sort of connection. This sort of easy comfort with a woman.

Clara fit Red Cedar Ranch like she belonged here. From the bond she'd formed almost immediately with his mother, to the way she cared for his daughters, Clara seemed to be the piece they'd been missing.

And he was feeling selfish.

His mother and daughters had her all week. He wanted to spend a little time with her himself. Get to know her better.

"I should stay with Wyatt." She started to back away, ready to put that distance she kept between them back in place.

But he was already over it. Tired of her trying to pretend like there was some reason they couldn't be alone.

They were both adults.

And contrary to what Clara believed, he was not her boss. Not directly.

Maryann Pace was in charge of Clara. He'd let his mother handle the process of selecting and hiring a nanny, and right now he was thanking God he had.

Because he would have never found Clara in a million years.

"I can promise you Wyatt will be begging to go to town

with them before breakfast is over." Brody risked a step closer, his finger itching to catch the bit of hair threatening to tangle in her dark lashes. "My parents will absolutely expect to take him with them."

"They don't have to do that."

"It's got nothing to do with having to, Clara." Brody tried to relax into the conversation, but it was almost impossible. All he could think of was how perfect she looked perched on his bed last night. Long hair pulled up at the top of her head in a messy knot. Soft pants hanging from her body like she'd worn them a hundred times. Dark-framed glasses perched on the raised bit just in the center of her nose as she read a story to his daughters and her son. "My parents will pull him into their orbit and take him on as another one of theirs." He paused. "If you'll let them."

It's the way his family had always been. Anyone came close to their gravitational pull and Maryann and Bill Pace latched on, doing their best to make them theirs forever.

It usually worked.

With one exception.

"That's very nice of them." Clara pulled another apple slice from the pocket at the front of her dress, holding it up for Edgar.

"It's not about being nice." Brody reached up to stroke the horse's neck. "It's how it is here. Family isn't just who you're born to."

A huffed out breath from the back of the barn snagged his attention.

Clara turned, following his line of sight. "Is that the horse that's pregnant?"

"Probably." Brody tipped his head toward where Penny's stall was. "Come on."

Clara only hesitated a second before following him. She only made it a few steps before her foot caught a little uneven spot in the dirt floor, making her stumble.

It was an opportunity he didn't plan to waste.

Brody grabbed her hand in his. "We're going to have to get you some boots if you're going to be out here." He led her down the center of the building, headed toward the back end where they had Penny set up in a foaling stall. The chestnut mare was clearly agitated. Enough Brody had to drop Clara's hand so he could go in and check her over, looking for any signs there might be a foal before the day's end. Her tail was sitting a little higher than normal, but other than that and her irritation, she didn't seem to be progressing. Brody ran one hand along her spine. "How ya doin' girl?"

Clara stood at the gate, peeking over the top into the stall. "Is there more straw in here?"

He stroked along Penny's side, checking to see how hard her belly was. "Most horses lay down to foal." He kicked around the straw. "This keeps her a little more comfortable."

Clara's eyes went wide as she eyed the space. "They just," she motioned toward where Penny stood, "lay down in here and push them out?"

"She'd probably rather run out in a field somewhere and do it, but we just don't have the manpower to let her do what she wants right now." Brody gave Penny one last swipe with his hand. It didn't seem like they'd be dealing with a birth today. "So she's stuck in here." He latched Penny's gate before taking Clara's hand in his. "Watch your step."

It was a weak excuse, but at this point he was willing to take anything he could get.

Not that he didn't realize sneaking closer to Clara was going to be a delicate balance. One he shouldn't even consider attempting.

He was going to do it anyway.

There might have been a chance he'd keep his distance, but the second he saw his daughters tucked tight, listening to Clara's soft voice reading to them, he knew there wasn't enough fight in him to make that happen.

As soon as they reached the barn door Clara pulled her hand from his, but stayed close. "When will she have her baby?"

"Maybe tomorrow." Brody glanced at the woman at his side. "Maybe the day after." He let his arm brush hers as they walked back toward the house. "You ever seen a foal?"

She gave a soft laugh. "Edgar is the first horse I've ever seen in real life."

"Good thing you came here then. You've been missing out." He eyed the pocket she'd filled with apples. "So has he."

Clara's eyes lifted to his as her fingers snagged the hair he'd wished he could touch, and tucked it behind one ear. "What does that mean?"

"Edgar's my mother's horse. He loves to go out on the ranch, but she hasn't been able to go out much lately. He's missing it." It was a dirty trick. One he should be ashamed of.

But there wasn't a lick of shame to be found right now. Whatever it took to get to steal her away he was willing to do.

Just to see if he was right.

See if Clara might be right for more than just Red Cedar Ranch.

"Mom." Wyatt raced from the back door, already dressed and bright-eyed. "Can I go with Maryann and Bill into town?"

It took all of a half second for Clara to peek his way out of the corner of her eyes. "What are they going into town for?"

"They're taking Leah and Michaela for lunch and ice cream." Wyatt's cheeks were pink as he beamed up at his mom. "They asked if I can go with them."

Brody leaned closer. "Told you."

Clara's elbow immediately jabbed into his ribs. "If you're sure they won't mind."

"I'm sure. I asked." Wyatt grabbed her around the waist in a tight hug. "Thank you." He squeezed Clara for a second before turning to race away, skidding to a stop before spinning back and lifting one hand. "Hey, Brody."

"Morning, Little Man."

Wyatt grinned as he spun away, running back up the stairs and into the house, calling out to whoever was in earshot. "She said yes."

"Looks like your afternoon just opened up."

Clara lifted her chin as she turned his way. "I don't have any boots."

Brody tipped her under the chin with one finger. "Don't need boots to ride, Darlin'." He let his gaze drift down the sundress swinging around her thighs. "Just a pair of pants." He let his finger slide over her skin. "It can even be the ones you wore to bed last night."

Her skin barely flushed, making him wonder if he wasn't the only one who struggled with their thoughts instead of sleeping last night. Clara jerked her chin off his finger. "I have other pants."

"I look forward to seeing them." He was toeing the line here. Coming dangerously close to pushing things too far too fast.

Clara's place in the house was set. Whatever happened, her position at Red Cedar Ranch was secure.

His was not. Maryann Pace wouldn't hesitate to banish him to the cabins at the other end of the hay barn, sending him off to sleep with the rest of the ranch hands if she decided he wasn't acting right.

It's where Boone had been since coming home. Probably where his brother was going to end up staying forever considering what it would take to get back in their mother's good graces.

"I'll think about it." Clara took a step toward the porch.

"Clara."

She paused, but didn't turn his way.

"It's just a ride. That's all." For now.

It was another heartbeat before she started walking again, without giving him any clue what she might be thinking about the parameters of their potential afternoon activities.

When he got inside there was no sign of Clara around the breakfast table. Saturday mornings the crowd was smaller. His mother fed the men Monday through Saturday, but most of the guys took Saturday morning off, sleeping in or going into town.

Brody snagged a plate of his own and got in line behind his brother Boone. Boone glanced his way. "What's wrong with you?"

He shook his head. "Not a thing."

Outside of the fact that he and Boone might soon be bunkmates.

"How's the new nanny doing?"

"The girls love her." It was the safest answer he could come up with for how things were going with Clara. "And she seems to love them back."

"What's not to love?" Boone grinned. "They set anything in her room on fire yet?"

"I hid all the lighters. She should be safe." Childproof igniters turned out to be not as proof as they advertised.

"You should probably give her a heads-up anyway." Boone scooped a pile of potatoes onto his plate.

Boone was the last of his brothers Brody expected to get helpful advice from. He'd managed to screw up his own relationship with one of the best catches in Moss Creek.

Hence his banishment to the cabins.

"I think I'll do that." Brody grabbed a couple biscuits, suddenly feeling much more optimistic about his intentions with Clara.

Not that he was completely positive what those were.

He just wanted to get to know her better. Spend a little time with the woman caring for his daughters.

Why should that be wrong?

"Damn."

Brody spooned some eggs onto his plate. "What's wrong?"

When Boone didn't answer him he glanced up.

And what was wrong became very clear.

Clara stood at the dining room table, a blonde little girl perched on each softly curved hip.

The pair of blue jeans painted onto her feminine frame did nothing to hide what her sundresses so successfully did.

Boone's grin turned deadly as he faced Clara's way.

Brody slapped one arm across his brother's chest. "I'll kick your ass right here in front of God and everybody."

CHAPTER SEVEN

THIS WAS A bad idea.

"Just take a deep breath." Brody's patience was unbelievable.

As was Edgar's. Her new horse friend stood there, all saddled up and ready to go, occasionally shooting her a skeptical look as she tried for the fifth time to get her ass up into the seat.

"I don't think I can do it." Clara tried to step back.

Why were horses so damn tall? It was like trying to hoist herself onto a moving platform, without sliding right over and off the other side.

Brody's hand pressed to the center of her back. "You can absolutely do it." He caught her hand and lifted it to where the reins still rested. "The first time is always the hardest."

Clara huffed out a frustrated breath, grabbing the reins and a clump of poor Edgar's hair with her left hand just like Brody showed her. Before she could lift her foot to the stirrup he moved in close.

"You want to make this one work?"

Of course she wanted to make this one work. Just like she wanted to make it work the last four times. She wanted to do this so much she was willing to be alone with Brody in order to do it. "Yes."

He chuckled. "I can give you a little boost."

Clara peeked over one shoulder. "What's that mean?"

"Means I can get your ass up in that saddle, but not without getting close."

The front of his body almost touched her back as it was. It was impossible to ignore.

Hell, it might be most of the reason she couldn't get on poor Edgar.

"Fine. Just do whatever it takes." She turned back to Edgar, angling her body toward his head as she reached up to grab the raised part at the back of the saddle.

When Brody first suggested taking her out for a ride she was ready to immediately reject the idea.

But the thought of knowing how to go out on her own someplace where she could finally just freaking breathe was too tempting to turn down.

"I'm ready whenever you are." Brody's hands settled onto her hips, strong and wide and warm.

Clara gritted her teeth over so many things and pushed up with her right foot, making sure to swing it high enough she didn't kick Edgar in the ass.

Again.

Brody's grip on her hips tightened, adding the additional boost she needed and stopping her from hesitating like she had before. Her butt settled into the worn leather of the saddle.

"I did it." She laughed a little. "Holy sh—" Her lips

clamped shut just in time, clipping off the word before it could escape.

Cursing was a slippery slope for her. One little *damn* and before you knew it there would be little blonde girls dropping F-bombs as they raced around the ranch.

Brody turned, looking from side to side at the men milling around the area. "Pretty sure the ranch hands don't mind if you say what you want, Darlin'."

Telling the father of the girls she'd been hired to help shape about her love of cursing was probably not a great idea.

But then neither was going out to a deserted part of the farm with him. "I try to keep it on a pretty tight leash so I don't say things when I shouldn't."

Brody reached down to check the length of the stirrups. "That must get pretty boring." He grinned up at her. "Everyone needs to let loose now and then."

She lifted one shoulder. "Not everyone has that luxury."

She'd been the only one taking care of Wyatt since the day he was born. At least for most of that time she didn't have the added burden of the financial and career worries that made her want to drop more than a few *fucks*.

Brody moved to Edgar's other side, checking the opposite stirrup. "Remember to relax." He reached up to adjust the reins. "Edgar knows what he's doing, so you shouldn't have to worry about too much."

Her stomach clenched a little as she looked around. Edgar seemed tall when she was standing on the ground, but it was nothing compared to now.

"Don't look down." Brody's hand rested on her thigh,

shaking it a little, dragging her attention back his way. "Doesn't matter how high you are."

"It seems like it does." She peeked over one side. "Hell."

Brody grinned. "There ya go." His hand stayed on her leg. "Let it out."

She sucked in a breath, straightening in the saddle.

Fake it till you make it.

"Let's go before I change my mind."

In the past year she'd had to do more things outside her comfort zone than in. She'd found an apartment. Gone back to school to finish the Early Childhood Education degree she never should have abandoned.

Found a job.

Moved states.

And she tackled each one of them the same way.

Fast. Before she could talk herself out of it.

Brody's horse was a few paces away, probably wondering what in the hell was taking so long. Brody was up and on the giant animal in a single move that was a hell of a lot more graceful than whatever maneuver it took to get her on Edgar. The horse immediately backed up, bringing Brody right to her side.

"How did you do that?" She eyed where his hands held the reins.

"Cowboy magic." He took the hat off his head and set it on hers. It immediately sank down loosely over her hair. "We need to get you a hat too."

Clara lifted her gaze to the brim shading her eyes. "You have a big head."

"Not the first time I've heard that one." His horse stepped

away and Edgar immediately followed, making her yelp in surprise. Brody's horse immediately stopped. "You okay?"

"Fine." She squeezed Edgar's reins in a death grip.

Brody's horse lined up with Edgar again. He reached over to take her hands in his, loosening her fingers. "He'll get confused if you start yanking on him."

"Sounds about right."

Clara blinked.

Did that come out of her mouth?

Brody's head dropped back as he laughed. "I'm going to have to get you away from the kids more often." He cupped his hands around hers with a light grip. "Like that."

She stared ahead, the heat of embarrassment creeping over her skin. "Got it."

"I know you do." His horse sidestepped away. "Are you ready?"

She didn't look at him. Couldn't. "Yup."

"Here we go then."

This time when Edgar started moving she was ready. Not that it made it any easier.

Every step Edgar took made his body sway, making her feel constantly off-balance as she rocked from side to side.

Brody stayed right at her side, watching.

He pressed one hand to his stomach. "Right here is what makes the difference." He patted what was probably a six-pack of stupidity. "Keep your belly tight. Use it to hold you steady."

Clara took a deep breath as she tried to figure out what in the hell he was talking about. She tried tensing her abs, but that just made her stiff and wobbly.

"Suck it in." Brody's stomach went even flatter under the tight fit of his blue t-shirt.

She laughed. Clearly he didn't realize sucking it in was a way of life for women who'd had children. "Got that covered, Cowboy."

Brody's horse slowed down and Edgar immediately followed suit as they moved farther from the house and barns. Clara did her best to hold her middle steady and it did seem to help, making it feel less like she was about to topple off and more like she was in a boat, rocking gently over the water.

Just in the middle of an open field.

"You're doing good."

"Thanks." She peeked Brody's way. "What's your horse's name?"

"Elvis."

Her head spun in his direction, the plan to keep her eyes to herself as much as possible forgotten instantly. "You're kidding."

"Nope." Brody was right at her side, making it easier to talk than she'd expected.

Hoped.

"My mom names all the horses. She likes short, sweet names better than long ones."

"You must like both."

"How's that?" He hadn't looked at where they were going in what seemed like a very long time.

"Leah and Michaela. One's short and sweet and one's long and flowing."

"Ah." He nodded his head in understanding. "Leah's mother chose her name."

"But not Michaela's?" It made her stomach squeeze to think that one daughter would have something so special from her mother and the other wouldn't."

"We each picked a name." Brody was quiet for a minute. "After Ashley died I changed my pick."

"Michaela wasn't the name you chose?"

Brody's eyes came to hers. "Michaela was Ashley's middle name."

The twist in her belly shifted, racing up to become a lump in her throat. "That will be important to her."

"I hope so." Brody reached over to once again loosen the death grip she had on Edgar's reins.

But this time it had nothing to do with fear.

She'd lost a lot, but it was nothing compared to what was ripped from Brody and his daughters. "I feel like I should tell you I'm sorry, but it doesn't seem to do the situation justice."

His hand lingered on hers. "Thank you." His horse bumped closer, bringing Brody's thigh almost to hers. "What about you?"

"What about me?" Everything she had to bitch about seemed trivial when it was set beside the sudden loss of a wife and new mother.

"What about your situation? What brought you here?"

"I guess Wyatt and I were just looking for a fresh start." She knew Brody probably wanted to discuss something besides his dead wife, but it still felt insensitive to take it much deeper than a surface-level explanation.

"That's all I get?" His tone was a little lighter. A little more relaxed. "I just dug deep for you."

"That's why that's all you get." She'd all but abandoned the reins. Like Brody promised, Edgar didn't need her input on the ride at all, so she ended up sliding her fingers down a bit of his mane. "You've been through something horribly painful." She rolled her head his direction. "I just got divorced." Mostly.

"If it was that simple you wouldn't be here, Darlin'." Brody squinted into the sun. "Why'd you come all the way to Montana?"

"I needed a job." She looked in the direction Brody was still looking. "Your mother offered me one so I took it."

The horses' trajectory changed, angling them toward whatever it was Brody was trying to better see. "I'm sure there's plenty of jobs you could have taken in California."

He wasn't completely wrong. "I guess this was an opportunity I couldn't pass up."

She and Maryann had clicked from the very beginning. That, combined with Cliff's glowing recommendation, was enough to make her willing to do whatever it took to get here.

In the end that included selling whatever they could, packing the rest in her little car and driving away from it all.

"Was Wyatt's father upset when you wanted to take him out of state?"

It was one more insult to add to injury. Whatever Richard did to her was fine.

The lying. The cheating. The manipulation.

But hurting Wyatt was something completely different.

"Unfortunately he didn't care." It was embarrassing to admit the type of man she'd given her son as a father. The type of man she'd been foolish enough to believe would always take care of her.

Turned out there's only one person in this world who will have your back no matter what.

You.

"I'm not sure that's as unfortunate as you think it is." Brody's words carried an edge to them. The same sort of tone he had the night they accidentally spent on the porch. "Wyatt might be better off without him in his life."

It was something she knew firsthand. The pain a damaged parent could cause. The fallout it could leave. "I keep trying to tell myself that."

"I'm happy to remind you whenever you want, Darlin'." The slow drawl of Brody's words registered, but not completely.

"What is that?" Clara peered across the field they'd been crossing. "Is it another house?"

"That is the reason my mother brought you here." Brody tipped his head toward the building that looked a lot like the family house behind them. "It's her little pet project."

"I don't know that I would call it little." Even from this far away it was easy to tell the place was at least twice as big as the main house. "What is it?"

"It's sort of a small-scale resort." Brody clicked his tongue and Elvis started moving faster.

Edgar immediately did the same. She'd just gotten used to the rhythm of riding at the pace they were going and this change felt like her teeth were rattling around in her head.

"Relax." Brody's body seemed to move perfectly in time with the horse while hers bounced a half-beat behind. "Get your legs under you. Same way they'd be if you were standing." He rested one hand on his stomach again. "Use your middle for balance."

Clara did her best to reposition herself as Edgar kept up with Elvis.

Fake it till you make it.

"Feet under me." She shifted her butt back a little, trying to figure out how to get everything lined up.

"There you go." Brody was still right at her side, his horse and Edgar perfectly pacing each other.

Her teeth stopped jamming into each other and the bang of the saddle into her lady basement eased.

To be fair it was the most action that particular part of her had seen in a long damn time.

In a few short minutes they were in front of the half-finished building.

"Come on." Brody easily swung his big body off Elvis' back, landing gracefully on his boots in the dirt.

"I'll just stay here." Getting on Edgar was difficult.

And in hindsight, probably a bad idea.

Because now she had to figure out how to get off at some point. But not this point.

"Come on." Brody held his hands up. "I want to show you the inside."

"But the outside is so pretty." Clara added a smile, hoping it would persuade him to get back on his horse and continue as they had been. Delay the inevitable for at least a little longer.

Brody shook his head. "Gotta get down sometime. Might as well be now."

She leaned away as he reached for her. "Or, it could be when we get back."

"You wanna have the ranch hands watch you try to get down for the first time?"

"Won't they be gone for the day?"

"Darlin', they came up with every excuse in the world to work around the house so they could watch you get on. I can promise you they'll be there to watch you get off." The smile froze on his face. "That came out wrong."

"You think?" At least she wasn't the only one making awkward, accidental innuendos. She dropped her head back and let out a loud sigh. "Why didn't you tell me I had to get off?"

"I thought that was always the goal?"

Her eyes snapped to his.

He gave her a wink. "Let's go. We've got shit to do."

"What do we have to do?"

"Well if I tell you then I don't have anything to bribe you off the horse with, now do I?" Brody motioned with his hands. "I promise I'll catch you. Leg up and over then come back toward me."

She did not want to do this here.

But she wanted to do it at the house in front of fifteen ranch hands less.

Clara lifted her butt out of the saddle, being careful not to be too rough as she moved her weight around, swinging her leg over and down, cringing as she started dropping toward the ground.

Brody's hands gripped her tight.

But something must have thrown him off, because her foot was not what hit the ground first.

Brody was.

CHAPTER EIGHT

HE'D NEVER BEEN less upset to land on his ass.

When Clara's swinging foot almost caught him in the balls, Brody's first reaction was to take a step back to avoid the impact.

It was a successful move.

But it also cost him the solid plant of his boots on the ground, resulting in both of them going to the dirt, Clara's soft body landing right on his as he held her close, hoping to keep her from the bulk of the impact. "You okay, Darlin'?"

Clara was completely silent and completely still.

Brody lifted his head up, trying to get a look at her face to make sure she wasn't hurt.

Her wide brown eyes stared up at Edgar. "I just fell off a horse."

He chuckled. "I'm not sure I'd say that."

Clara tipped her head his way. "You said you'd catch me."

"I've got you, don't I?"

Her eyes barely widened, slowly moving down to where

his arms still held her tight. "Crap." Clara immediately tried to roll away.

"Hang on." Brody pushed up to a sitting position, hoping to give her a better start.

And trying to keep her close a few seconds longer. "You probably don't want to roll around out here."

Clara pushed free of his hold, immediately crawling away from him. "I probably don't want to be lying on top of you in a field more."

"I could choose to be offended by that." Brody bent one knee and slung his arm over it as he watched her.

She pushed to her feet, dusting off the dirt and dried vegetation covering the jeans he'd been struggling to ignore.

But for what? To try to pretend he didn't find her attractive?

It was a damn near impossible thing to accomplish.

"There's nothing to be offended by." She straightened, looking him right in the eye. "I'm your daughters' nanny. That's it."

"What if you weren't my daughters' nanny?" It was something he'd been struggling with himself.

How to figure out what might be between them without going too far.

His daughters loved her already. His mother adored her.

Losing Clara over his own selfishness wasn't an option.

She gave him a little shrug. "It doesn't matter." Her eyes held his. "I need this job, Brody. I worked hard to get it."

"And I can promise you no matter what you'll keep it." He risked a step closer to her. "The only way you won't have this job is if you choose to not have it."

She laughed softly. "I think you're missing how easily I could be left with no other choice."

Damn. He thought maybe today could be the day he found his way under the skin of armor Clara strapped on each morning to keep him at bay.

Brody dropped his head in a nod. "Understood."

He lifted his eyes to the building in front of them. "You still interested in seeing the inn?"

"I'm not saying I don't want to have anything to do with you, Brody." Clara let out a little breath. "I just think it's best if we both recognize what this can never be."

It wasn't what he was hoping to hear, but it was understandable. "I want what you want." He reached his hand out. "Friends it is."

Clara gave him a smile as her shoulders relaxed. She took his hand in a firm shake. "Friends." She looked to the inn. "Now show me around."

They spent an hour going through the half-completed inn and the space around it. Clara seemed to be genuinely interested in their plans for the place and asked enough questions to keep the conversation flowing and easy.

By the time they were ready to saddle up she was smiling more than he'd seen.

She stood at Edgar's side and took a deep breath.

"You can do it."

She turned his way, giving him a smile that dug his disappointment deeper. "I know." Clara grabbed the reins and saddle just like he'd shown her, and in one mostly-coordinated move, managed to get her ass settled into the saddle. She beamed down at him. "I did it."

"I knew you could." Brody mounted up and turned to her. "You think you're ready to go a little faster?"

Her eyes lit up as Clara rolled her lips inward pressing them tightly together. She gave him a little nod.

"Keep your feet under your hips and barely lift your butt out of the saddle and you'll be just fine." He gave her a wink. "Hold onto your hat."

Clara's eyes rolled upward. "It's your hat."

He knew damn well it was his hat perched on her head. Something about it settled the unrest caused by her unwillingness to even consider they might have a connection that warranted more than friendship. "And it's my favorite one, so make sure it stays right where it is."

Brody gave her a second to prepare before urging Elvis to a slow trot, staying close enough he could help Clara work through what he and his brothers had done so long it was second nature.

It was his other reason for taking her out today. Soon they'd be facing down a whole slew of inexperienced riders, and teaching them quickly was essential to their horses' happiness. "Move with him. Follow along with how he moves."

Clara's brows came together as she focused, her behind slowly starting to lift and lower with the pattern of Edgar's trot.

He gave her some time to get adjusted before pushing Elvis to go a little faster.

Clara's eyes widened but that was her only reaction to the change in pace.

"Lean forward a little more. It'll help keep you balanced."

She immediately did as he suggested, her body moving

into what would be a comfortable pose for both Clara and the horse.

Brody urged Elvis a little faster, to a full gallop, watching Clara and Edgar closely.

If it was possible for a horse to smile, then Edgar was. He looked almost as happy as the woman on his back. Clara's hair blew around her shoulders and her smile was wide and pure.

Unfortunately, Edgar hadn't been out much lately, and letting the horse push too hard too fast was a risk Brody wouldn't take. Not even to keep seeing that smile on her face.

Brody slowed Elvis down. His horse immediately backed off.

Edgar however, didn't seem to be done. The gelding continued on, racing across the open field.

"Shit." Brody nudged Elvis, bringing his own horse back up to speed. He'd only taught Clara the most basic commands, assuming Edgar would be like he always was.

Looked like Clara was a bad influence on him.

Her head turned to one side before snapping back his way.

Edgar almost immediately started to slow, his gallop easing to a reluctant stop.

Clara was smiling wide as Brody finally caught up to her. "I remembered how to tell him to stop."

Edgar huffed out a snort, shaking his head at the command he definitely didn't want to follow.

But still did.

Clara's eyes were shining and her cheeks were pink. She looked so different from the careful, quiet woman he couldn't help but want to get closer to.

And that was before he saw this side of her.

This side of Clara deepened the ache of loneliness he'd been feeling lately. Pulled it to the surface like nothing else had.

"I think you might be a natural." He wanted that for her. Wanted Clara to feel confident doing something she might end up loving as much as he did.

She rolled her eyes. "You already forgot about me falling off then."

He definitely hadn't forgotten. The feel of her body against his would haunt him long after this day was over. "Everyone falls off a horse sometime." Brody reached out to flick the brim of his hat. "The key is to get your ass back up and try again."

"Isn't that the truth." Clara's body moved along with each step Edgar took, making her look like a woman who'd been on a horse more than just once.

"I take it you've done a lot of getting back up."

"You could say that." She glanced his way before turning to look out over the grassland around them. "My soon-to-be-ex-husband left me pretty high and dry."

"I'd sort of put that together." Brody tried to keep the edge out of his tone, but it was hard. "Not sure how a man can do that to his family."

Clara shrugged. "I don't know that he considers us his family at this point." Her lips moved to a sad smile. "He seems to think that's something that can be replaced."

If he'd hated Dick before then that comment moved it to full-on loathing. Richard Rowe better hope their paths never crossed, because only one of them would come out of it upright.

"Sometimes I think I shouldn't be so mad about it." Clara continued on. "Wyatt deserves better."

"So do you."

"What I deserve doesn't really matter."

"It should." Brody knew this was edging into dangerous territory. Coming close to the lines Clara believed should stay between them.

"That's not how parenting works." She turned his way. "You know that. I've seen how you are with your girls. You will always put them first."

"Sometimes putting yourself first *is* putting them first." It was a conclusion he'd come to in the recent past. "Sometimes you have to make yourself happy to make them happy." For a long time finding a partner for himself seemed selfish. Like the time he would spend finding someone to be at his side would take time from his daughters.

And it would.

But it would be for the greater good.

Clara gave him a little smile. "I think we might have to agree to disagree on that one."

"That's only because you've never been in a good relationship."

Clara scoffed. "How do you know that?"

"You wouldn't be here if you had." Brody edged Elvis closer to Edgar, leaving only as much space between them as he had to. "And you sure as hell wouldn't be arguing with me about what seeing you in a happy relationship could do for your son."

It was a big part of what he wanted for his girls. For them to see how a man should treat a woman. For them to grow up expecting it. Right now his parents were all they had as an example, and that just wasn't close enough to really drive it home.

"It's not nearly what it would do to him seeing me in another bad relationship." Clara's head tipped down. "He's seen that too much already."

"Then you have the chance to show him something different. Show him how it's supposed to be."

Her eyes came his way, one brow lifted. "I feel like you're pleading your case."

"Not mine." He leaned back a little, taking Elvis a few paces away. "Just your son's."

Clara turned away, falling silent as they continued across the growing grass, back toward the main house.

As he expected, every hand on the ranch was there when they got back, faking like they had work to do. Waiting to see Clara.

Hopefully she had the same rules for everyone else, otherwise he'd have to make it clear she was off limits.

And she was.

Brody stopped Elvis just beside the barn, expecting Clara to wait for him to help her off Edgar.

But before his boots hit the ground she was lifting up in the seat and swinging one leg up and over, her body dropping toward the ground.

Brody darted around Elvis's backside, ready to scoop her up before either horse could sidestep her direction. Clara smirked his way, both her feet firmly planted in the grass. "Something wrong, Cowboy?"

"You did a real good job gettin' off that horse." Brooks came around Edgar's rear. "You have a nice ride?"

"It was fine.' Clara gave Brooks a tight smile, her spine as straight as an arrow. "If you'll excuse me. I should probably get cleaned up before the girls get back." She pushed between Brody and his brother and made straight for the house.

Brooks turned to watch her go, one arm slung over Edgar's back. "You ask Boone if he's got space for your ass in his cabin?"

"Shut up." Brody went to work on his horse. Luckily the slow walk home was enough to cool Edgar and Elvis down, but there was still tack to remove. Thank God, since his afternoon with Clara gave him more to chew on than he might be prepared to handle and he needed the time to digest.

"I dunno." Brooks shook his head. "That one might be worth ending up in a cabin over."

"It's not just about the damn cabin." Brody removed Elvis's bridle as his younger brother did the same to Edgar. "She's perfect for the girls. They love her. I can't risk that."

"If she's so perfect with the girls then—"

"Once again, shut up." It was something he'd thought of at least a million times since Clara arrived.

"So your plan is to just stand around and wait for her to find someone else in town?" Brooks stared at him over Edgar's back. "Cause I can guarantee you there's at least twenty men around here willing to do whatever it takes to snag her."

"Not necessarily." It was another of the things he'd thought of a million times. "Wouldn't take much to deter anyone who thinks they deserve her."

"So you won't put your ass on the line to try to have her yourself, but you'll threaten anyone else's who *is* willing?"

That was pretty much it. "It's not my ass that's on the line." Brody hefted the saddle off and headed to the barn. "I don't want her to be uncomfortable here."

He wanted to do whatever it took for Clara to stay. For his girls to have her even if he couldn't.

And for Clara to have what she so desperately wanted and needed.

Brody paused as his father's truck came down the lane and parked in its usual spot. He could hear his girls hollering before they were even free of their car seats. He turned to face them, plastering on a smile as he waited.

But neither girl even looked his way. Both little blondes ran straight for the house, screaming for Clara at the top of their lungs.

"Damn." Brooks shook his head. "That's bad, man."

"Told you." Brody was about to head to the barn when he realized there was one set of eyes on him.

Wyatt stood at the edge of the truck, quietly watching.

"Hey, Little Man." Brody tipped his head toward the barn. "You wanna come help us?"

Wyatt's face lit up immediately. "Really?"

"You might as well learn how to be a cowboy since this is your home now." The more Brody learned about Dick and his fucked-up ways, the more his heart broke for Wyatt. The kid deserved to have a man in his life that had his back no matter what.

Maybe he could be that.

And maybe it would make having Clara so close and still so far a little easier to bear.

CHAPTER NINE

"WHAT'S MATTER?" LEAH stared up at her, eyes wide. "Your face looks weird."

Clara worked to pull her eyes from the scene outside the kitchen window. "I'm fine."

"Did you fart? That's how Mmm-kayla look when she farts."

"I didn't fart."

"Who taught you that word?" Maryann stood at the counter, her head turned their way.

Both girls' lips pressed tight together.

"Here." Clara passed out the lidded cups she was supposed to be filling instead of watching Brody and her son together in the yard for the fifth day in a row. "I want you to drink all of that before lunch."

Michaela stared at the cup Clara held. "I'm not firsty."

"Water keeps our bodies healthy. You want to grow big and strong so you can skydive, right?"

It was the girls' newest obsession. They'd seen a

commercial for a local company that offered skydiving and they hadn't stopped talking about it since.

Thank God it had a weight and age limit Clara could use to her advantage.

So did zip-lining and parasailing. Two more things the girls thought sounded amazing.

Michaela took the cup and immediately sucked down a few gulps before following her sister into the front room for their daily watching of *Barbie Goes Scuba Diving*.

Apparently Barbie was the adventurous type.

"I'm a little concerned you might have a couple adrenaline junkies on your hands." Clara turned back to the sink to rinse out the girls' breakfast dishes. They'd slept in and missed the ranch breakfast Maryann made each morning.

Which worked out for Clara. Meant she could skip it too and avoid the temptation that was Brody Pace.

She'd laid down the law and now had to stick to it.

Especially since he seemed to be.

Which didn't disappoint her at all.

"Awe. Look at that." Maryann wiped her hands on a towel as she looked out the same window Clara was supposed to be ignoring.

But not looking now would be rude.

She almost winced as she turned her eyes to peek outside.

It was going to be bad. She could feel it.

"He's taken to that like a fish to water." Maryann's smile was wide as she watched Brody lead Edgar around the yard, Wyatt perched on the horse's back in the hat and boots that somehow appeared one day.

"Shit." It came out on the next exhale.

Maryann immediately turned her way. "What's wrong, Dear?"

"Oh." Clara blinked a few times. "I forgot to pay my car insurance." She backed away. "I should go do that now."

Clara raced up the stairs to the room where she was staying, dropping her butt to the bed and catching her head in her hands.

Brody was making her lose her mind.

It was hard enough looking at the man in his flipping jeans and boots all day, walking around in damn t-shirts that were just a little too tight and always had a smudge of dirt somewhere, proving he'd been working hard.

But then she had to deal with him taking care of his daughters. Cuddling them. Tickling them. Keeping his sanity when they managed to stack enough random things to climb on the shelf where the lighters were hidden.

And now...

For the love of God, now she had to watch him with her son. Treating Wyatt the way she'd always wished his own father would.

Something had to be done.

Something drastic.

And it had to happen now.

Clara pushed up from the bed and hurried back down the stairs.

"Did you see me?" Wyatt stood at the bottom, his cowboy hat still perched on his head. "I rode Edgar."

"I saw." She shoved on a smile. "You did such a good job."

"That's what Brody said." Wyatt beamed up at her. "He said maybe I can get my own horse since Edgar's yours."

Her head started tilting on its own volition. "Is that what he said?"

Wyatt nodded.

"Great. That's amazing." Her face was frozen in place, the smile she wore almost painful as she contemplated figuring out how to string Brody Pace up by his boots from the rafters of the barn. "Why don't you go get cleaned up and ready for lunch?"

As Wyatt hustled up the stairs she turned toward the back of the house. Maryann and the girls were in the living room watching the last fifteen minutes of scuba Barbie as she passed by.

The door to the barn was open and she went straight in, finding Brody wiping down the saddles lined inside. "You." Clara pointed one finger at him. "Stop it."

Brody glanced her way, lifting a brow. "Saddles got to be maintained, Darlin'."

"You know what I'm talking about." She went straight up to him. "And stop with the *Darlin'* thing too."

He turned to face her. "What's got you all riled up?"

"You do." Clara waved her hands around his front. "You and your whole existence."

Brody was making this harder than it had to be, and right now she was pretty sure he was doing it on purpose.

"My existence has you upset." Brody's head tipped down just enough that his hat shaded his eyes. "Not much I can do about that one, D—" His lips lifted in a little smirk. "Clara."

Her name rolled off his tongue, the drawl he always had seeming more pronounced than usual.

Her eyes snapped open wide. "You *are* doing this on purpose."

"Still not sure what you're talking about."

"You are trying to make me like you."

"I would hope you like me. You take care of my daughters, and I'd think you hating me would be a problem."

If she was mad before coming out here, then he just turned it to full-on fury. "Stop pretending to be innocent."

Brody took a step closer to her, the scent that was burned into her brain coming with him. "I can promise you, I'm anything but innocent, Clara."

Her breath caught as he eased in a little more. "And I won't apologize for spending time with Wyatt." His head shook just a little. "I don't care how it makes you feel. And I don't give a shit if it makes you like me. That's your problem, not mine."

Screw stringing him up. She was going to kill him. Murder Brody Pace right inside his own barn. "If you hurt my son—"

His head dipped, the brim of his hat so close it nearly touched her forehead. "If you were about to suggest I would ever cause Wyatt the kind of pain his father has then you and I are going to have the sort of problems you were worried about." His blue eyes were dark as they held hers. "That little boy needs to see that there are men out there who will put him first. Men who don't have to be his blood to do it."

Clara glared at him, trying to keep the rage burning in her belly.

He stared her down, blue gaze unwavering.

"Damn it, Brody." She grabbed his shirt with both hands, fisting it tight.

She wasn't normally impulsive.

Maybe it was the heat of the moment.

Maybe it was temporary insanity.

Whatever it was that made her do it, she would have to come to terms with it later.

Because somehow, she accidentally pulled Brody Pace's lips to hers.

It was something she'd considered more times than she could count and certainly more than she should admit.

That might be why it happened. Her brain finally short circuited and went into autopilot, acting out its most popular reel.

Before that same brain could wrap itself around their current predicament, her back was pressed tight to the side of Edgar's stall with Brody's broad body pinning her in place as his hands came to her face. The rasp of his fingers against her skin was nothing her imagination could have come up with on its own, and would certainly be added to the guilty fantasy she pretended didn't exist.

Clara might have started the kiss, but her ownership of the act was fleeting. In a heartbeat she was at his mercy, unable to do anything but follow where he led.

Because his hands weren't the only thing she never could have imagined.

Everything about Brody was foreign to her, and that included the way his mouth moved over hers. It was firm and sure, but so careful.

Somehow possessing without taking.

His lips trailed over her skin, sliding against the line of her jaw toward her ear where his teeth nipped at her skin. "You taste just like I knew you would."

Her stomach flipped in a way she hadn't felt in so long it

was almost painful. "Why were you thinking about how I would taste?"

"I agreed to your rules, Darlin', but keeping you out of my thoughts wasn't one of them." His mouth skimmed down her neck. "Which I appreciate more than you would believe." One wide palm moved down her center, sliding between her breasts and over her belly before easing around her body to cup the curve of her ass, pulling her tight to him.

The low groan that passed through the lips still pressed to her skin shot straight to her core, warming places she'd long abandoned.

"Brody, I—" Clara's breath caught as the fingers of his other hand forked into the hair at the nape of her neck, pulling tight to angle her head back as his mouth once again covered hers, swallowing down any argument she might have managed to drum up.

And there wasn't much.

She knew staying away from him would be her only saving grace. Knew if she didn't keep distance between them it would all go to shit.

And here she was. Standing in a pile of shit, struggling to care that she was sinking fast.

But it wasn't just her that would go down with the ship.

"I can't." The words were almost painful to push out.

Brody immediately froze, his head lifting until his eyes met hers. The loss of his lips on her skin left it cold. Abandoned.

He didn't say a word, just waited.

She should tell him this was a mistake.

It was.

She should tell him it couldn't happen again.

It couldn't.

She should tell him she was sorry.

She was not.

"Damn it, Brody." Clara wrapped her arms around his neck, pulling his lips back to hers and knocking his hat to the ground.

The sound of tires on the gravel drive sent her spine snapping straight and reality crashing down.

"Relax." Brody held her tight as he leaned to peek around Edgar's stall and out the still-open door. His brows lifted. "It's the mail carrier."

Clara let out a little breath as Brody stepped away, grabbing his hat and setting it on his head before pressing his hand to her back and easing her toward the door. Maryann stood on the porch, her brows drawn together as the woman from the post office gestured to the item in her hand.

"Is something wrong?" Maryann didn't look happy and Brody was acting strange.

"We pick our mail up in town. It's a long haul out here for them and it's easier for us." Brody lifted one hand as the woman looked their way. "Hey there, Sharon. What brings you all the way out here?"

Sharon turned, her face falling when she saw Clara. "Hey, Brody." She held up the envelope she'd been waving around a minute ago. "Are you Clara Rowe?"

Maryann's lips turned down in a frown.

Clara glanced Brody's way before looking back toward where Sharon continued coming their way. "Yes."

Sharon scrunched her aging face up as she passed the envelope Clara's way. "I have certified mail for you." She held out a three-layer form the size of a half sheet of paper. "I need you to sign for it."

Clara took the pen Sharon offered, doing her best to sign across her flattened palm before passing it back. "Thank you."

"You might not want to thank me yet." Sharon tipped her head toward the mail. "It's from an attorney in California. Nothing good ever comes from attorneys in California."

Clara took the letter, doing her best to manage a smile for the woman in front of her. "I'm sure it will be fine."

Sharon reached out to pat Clara's shoulder. "Good girl. Don't let anyone give you shit." She turned, lifting one arm high in a wave. "Bye, Mer. See you Sunday for bridge."

Maryann nodded back, her eyes quickly coming back Clara's way as Sharon piled back into her car and turned to head out. "You okay, Dear?"

"Yup." Clara started to wobble a little on her feet as the fear she tried to get used to chewed on her insides.

What in the hell did Dick want to take from her now? There was nothing left. Nothing else he could claim complete ownership of.

Maryann watched her a second longer before her eyes slid to Brody, hanging on her son a second before she turned and went into the house.

"What do you think it is?"

"With Dick the dick there's no telling." Clara ripped into the envelope, wanting to get it over with.

"I think I might be wearing off on you, Darlin'." Brody's hand rested on her back, warm and wide. A steady presence to ground her while the world was spinning too fast.

Because Sharon was right. Certified mail was never a

good thing. "He is a dick." She worked so hard not to say anything disparaging about Wyatt's father in front of him.

Even though some days it was physically painful not to call him what he was.

A dick.

Clara pulled the papers free of the envelope. As she scanned the pages, the bite of fear turned to something else.

Sickness.

"You've got to be kidding me." She blinked hard, trying to clear what had to be the wrong words.

"What's wrong?" Brody came closer, his body lining up against hers as the hand on her back moved to pull her into his side.

She swallowed the saliva collecting in her mouth, trying to ease the gag reflex tightening her throat.

Wyatt would be devastated. Completely heartbroken by what Richard was claiming.

All in the name of money.

"Does that say he wants a paternity test?" Brody's voice rose with every word that came out of his mouth. "Is he fucking serious?"

Clara pressed her lips together. "It seems like he is."

"Why in the hell would he do that to Wyatt?" Brody's grip on her tightened. "To you?"

She took a slow breath, fighting through her own discomfort. "Because he knows I won't do it."

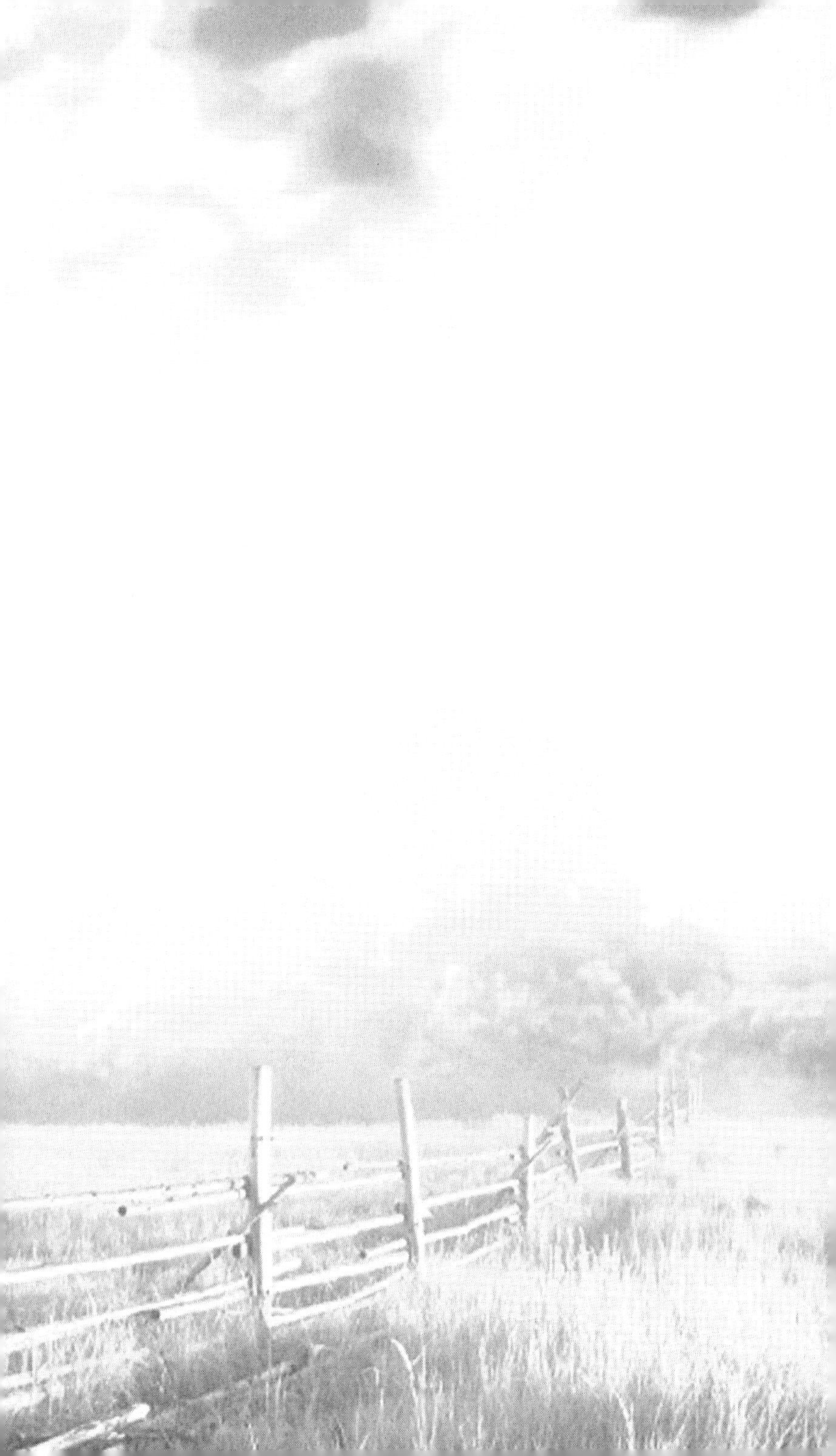

CHAPTER TEN

"HOW'S SHE DOING?" His mother came to stand at his side, watching out the window to where Clara stood at Edgar's side, brushing along his coat with a curry comb.

"She's pissed." She might not even know it, but Clara was most definitely angry. "She's trying to figure out how to not be."

His mother crossed her arms, frowning out at the woman they both were partial to. "That doesn't make any sense."

"It does when you remember she's used to doing it all on her own. If she was mad there was no way to keep Wyatt from knowing. No one else to occupy him while she worked through it."

Maryann shook her head. "It breaks my heart. She's the sweetest girl."

"She'll get there." Brody started to step away.

"Brody Pace, you better be watching yourself."

He knew it was coming sooner or later. His mother paid attention to everything that happened at Red Cedar Ranch, and it was only a matter of time before she realized what was going on between him and Clara.

And there was definitely something going on.

Finally.

"I don't plan on sharing a bunk with Boone if that's what you're saying."

His mother shook her head, hands on her hips. "You'll be lucky to share a bunk with Boone if you do anything to cause that girl a second of upset." She pointed toward the back of the property where the inn was under construction. "They've still got to pour the cement for the back patio."

"Boone breaks Mae Wells' heart and still gets to live on the ranch, but you're going to bury me under concrete?"

"Boone is suffering for what he did." She pointed one finger Brody's way. "And Mae can handle what happened. Clara doesn't need any more hell thrown her way."

"And that's what you think I'll do? Throw hell her way?" He'd been alone so long and now it seemed like everyone was out to block his path to potential happiness.

"That's not what I said." His mother snapped it out. "But Clara needs someone to look out for her, and I will do whatever it takes to make sure she can finally enjoy her life." Maryann's eyes narrowed on his. "Did you know she worked two jobs while going to school, trying to make enough money to take care of her son?"

He didn't know that, but it didn't surprise him.

"Miss Maryann?" Wyatt walked into the kitchen, clamping Brody's lips shut. "Have you seen my mom?"

"Your mom is helping take care of Edgar for me right now." Brody stepped in front of the window. Clara needed time to deal with the letter from the attorney and he intended to give it to her. "You wanna go with me to check out the Inn?"

Wyatt's eyes brightened. "Sure."

Brody fished his keys from his pocket and went for the front door, leading Wyatt away from where Clara was. "I need to make sure everything's where it needs to be." He opened the front door and let Wyatt go out first. "They're supposed to be digging out for the pool today."

"There's going to be a pool?" Wyatt's gaze was wide.

"And a hot tub." They'd gone back and forth on whether or not to put the pool in right away, or if they actually needed one at all. At the end of the day, his family wanted the Inn at Red Cedar Ranch to be something special. They wanted to attract people who were used to nice things, which meant they had to offer nice things.

"Can I swim in the pool when it's done?"

"We're all swimming in the pool when it's done, Little Man."

Wyatt grinned at him from the passenger's seat, holding tight to the hat on his head as the wind blew in through the open truck window.

As Brody expected, the backhoe was there when they pulled up to the construction site, digging out the pool and spa area at the back of the inn.

Wyatt climbed out of the truck, gaze fixed on the building. "That place is huge."

"Hopefully we can keep it full of people." It was the biggest fear he had about this whole venture.

What if no one came?

Then they'd dropped an amount of money that threatened to make him choke almost every time he looked at it, and ended up with nothing to show for it outside of an empty building and a pool no one but their family used.

"Everyone will want to come here." Wyatt stood in his jeans and boots, hands on his hips as he looked around him. "It's the best place I've ever been."

"I'm glad to hear that." Brody tipped his head toward the area where the pool was going in. "Let's go make sure everything's going the way it should be."

Wyatt stuck right by his side, listening as he spoke with the project foreman about permits and timelines. After what had to be the most boring hour Wyatt ever spent, they were finally loaded back into the truck and heading to the house. As they passed the line of cabins where the ranch hands stayed Wyatt pointed toward them. "What are those?"

"Those are where the people who work here live." He left Boone out of the explanation to keep it simple.

"My mom works here."

So much for a simple explanation.

He could tell Wyatt the reason why he and his mother started out in the house. Explain that it was easiest for everyone if Clara was close to the girls she was watching, but he settled on the most current reason. "Your mom's special."

Wyatt didn't miss a beat. "I know." He turned Brody's way, his brows coming together under the brim of his hat. "Why do *you* think she's special?"

"She's a good mom."

The crease between Wyatt's brows deepened. "She's the best mom." His eyes stayed on Brody as he waited for more reasons.

Brody shifted in his seat. It hadn't occurred to him that

Maryann might not be his biggest threat in this situation. "And she's smart, and strong, and kind."

Wyatt's eyes narrowed as he continued to stare Brody down. "She's pretty too."

"Definitely pretty." Pretty didn't come close to describing Clara, but he probably shouldn't try to argue that point right now. "And a hard worker."

"She worked all the time after we had to move." Wyatt still watched him. "She worked at the restaurants and did school work and took care of me."

"You're a wise kid, you know that, Little Man?" Most children didn't realize their care was hard work. Even fewer acknowledged it.

"My mom says that." Wyatt's lips edged down in a frown. "But she doesn't look happy when she says it."

It made sense. "Wisdom doesn't come from living an easy life, Buddy. Your mom is sad that your life hasn't been easy."

"I don't want her to be sad."

Brody reached over to squeeze Wyatt's shoulder. "Me either."

"EDGAR'S GOING TO make room for you in his stall if you spend any more time out here." Brody leaned against the open door to the barn.

Clara stood at the gate to Edgar's stall in her pajamas, the length of her dark hair tied up at the top of her head, the glasses she only wore at night perched on her nose. "I couldn't sleep."

"I figured." He walked inside. "You been back to check on Cricket yet?"

Her lips curved into a small smile. "Maybe."

His mother had claimed to be too busy to come up with a name when the new foal was born, passing the naming of the newest addition to the stable off onto Clara. "She's really cute."

"They always are." Brody headed back to where Penny and her baby were both resting. Cricket was curled up in the deep straw and Penny was dozing close by. She shook her head as he approached, quickly coming to the gate. "How you doing, momma?"

Clara came in close at his side, holding out one of the apple snacks he started buying by the pallet to be sure she never ran out. "She's a good momma."

He reached out to scratch Penny's cheek as the horse crunched through her snack. "It's a hard thing to be."

Clara sighed. "What in the hell am I supposed to do about the paternity test?" Her head dipped a little. "Wyatt's old enough to know what's going on. If I don't do it then Dick can try to claim he's not Wyatt's father and shouldn't have to help support him."

"Does he support him now?"

She snorted out a single, bitter laugh. "He's supposed to pay five hundred dollars a month, but he knows exactly how much he has to give me in order to stay out of trouble." She shook her head. "He always sends a partial payment right before we have a court date."

"Is it worth it?"

Clara rolled the remaining treat in her hand between her fingers, staring down at it as she did. "It's hard because I feel like letting him wipe us from his life makes me look weak. I feel like I should hold him accountable. Make him take care of the responsibilities he has." Her eyes lifted to his. "I mean, the money would have been nice over the past year, but now it's not even about that."Clara's gaze leveled. "I want him to pay for what he did to Wyatt one way or another."

A flicker of rage flashed through her eyes, giving him a glimpse of the woman Clara kept hidden from most people. Brody reached up to slide his fingers down the side of her face. "People like Dick always pay. It might not look the way we want it to, but I promise you, he will suffer for what he did to you and Wyatt."

Her brows lifted. "Are you about to say something about how someday he'll realize he lost the best thing he ever had?" Her lips almost lifted at the corners. "Because that would be about the most cliché thing you could possibly come up with."

"I was going to say he'll probably end up with hemorrhoids from being such a tight ass." Brody relaxed a little at the softening of Clara's expression. Knowing she was struggling and there was nothing he could do about it bothered him. He eased closer, wanting to feel her against him. "But now that you mention it—"

She held one hand up. "Don't say it. I'll never be able to look at you the same."

"Oh, I see how you look at me, Darlin'." Brody grabbed her as she laughed, the light sound filling the silent barn. "And it might be good for my sanity if you looked at me a little different."

"It's those damn shirts." She pressed her hands into the

fabric of the t-shirt he'd changed into after his shower. "Do you not own anything looser?"

"If I do I can promise you'll never see it." He pressed against her, urging her feet back. "I might even burn them just to be sure."

"That's just mean." Clara's smile held, her expression softer than it had been since she got that damn letter.

From the Dick.

"Did you think I was a nice guy?" He pushed against her as Clara's back rested against the side of Penny's stall.

Clara's eyes dipped to where her hands still rested against his chest. "You are a nice guy." Her fingers moved over his pecs, tracing his skin through the fabric with a soft touch. "Thank you for taking Wyatt with you today."

"You deserved a minute to deal with what happened without having to worry about pretending everything was fine." He reached up to stroke down the side of her face, brushing one thumb across her cheek.

Her eyes lifted to his. "Why do you have to be like this? It's really not what I was hoping for when I came here."

Brody smiled down at her. "Sorry to mess all your plans up."

"You did." Clara was back to smoothing her hands over his chest, this time with a slightly bolder touch. "You're a huge problem for me." Her fingers dipped lower, sliding across his stomach. "I'm sure it's mostly these shirts you keep wearing."

"Probably, but like I said, I don't plan on wearing anything else." He leaned closer, breathing in the soft scent of her skin. "Might even find some that are tighter, just to see what'll happen."

"I think I might have to take back what I said about you being a nice guy." Her lips pressed tight, but still couldn't hide the smile fighting for a place there.

"I am a nice guy, Darlin'." He ran his nose along her neck. "But I'm also a hell of a man."

Clara inhaled sharply as Brody caught the lobe of her ear between his teeth, her hands gripping his shirt as his lips found the spot just below it.

"I love the way you smell." If sunshine after the rain had a smell it would be this. Warm and soft and bright in spite of what came before. He nipped her skin again. "I love the way you taste."

"I wish you didn't." Her body pushed a little tighter to his as his lips dipped lower, skimming along the bit of collarbone peeking out from the neck of her well-worn shirt.

He caught the hem of it with one hand, tucking his fingers under it to find the satiny soft of her skin. "Do you really wish that, Clara?" Brody trailed his touch up her side. "Do you really wish I didn't lay at night thinking about you?" Her body was bare under the shirt, no bra to act as a barrier between them. Brody carefully stroked over her ribs, giving Clara time to realize his intent.

Time to stop him.

Because as much as he tried to convince himself differently, this was dangerous territory.

Every step they took would make it all the more difficult if Clara decided to hit the brakes, leaving him to stand in the background of her life, wishing he could be at her side.

Her back arched toward him as she pressed closer. "Thinking about me at night doesn't do anyone any good." The pads of her fingers raked over the skin of his stomach as her hands found their way under his shirt. "It will just make you crazy."

"Is that what happens to you, Clara?" He'd never considered she might be doing the same two doors down. "You think of me at night and it makes you crazy?" Brody ran his hand across her ribs again, dragging them just below the swell of her breasts.

"I don't want to talk about it." She whimpered a little as his hand teased the underside of one softly-rounded mound. "And if you're just going to tease me I'm going to bed."

CHAPTER ELEVEN

SHE'D LOST HER mind. It was out on the ranch somewhere, running amuck.

Leaving her to cause problems of her own.

The main one being Brody Pace and the flat plane of the belly she couldn't seem to figure out how to keep her hands off of.

"Is that what you think this is? Me teasing you?" His hand immediately came to cover her breast, rolling the nipple between his calloused fingers. "I was trying to give you time to get used to the idea of us being together, Clara." His hand shoved her shirt up, the air of the barn barely reaching her skin before his mouth closed around her other nipple.

She knew she was taunting him.

That's what made it such a problematic move. There was only one real outcome for the words she let herself say.

And she knew it as she said them.

Her head fell back against the stall behind her, eyes falling closed as Brody's hands and mouth gave her what she'd spent too many nights imagining. When his mouth finished on one side it moved to the other, his tongue and teeth raking against her with an amount of skill that might land her ass on the barn floor if she wasn't careful.

Brody pressed harder against her, his weight adding support to her sagging knees. His mouth dropped her breast and came to cover hers in a kiss that started with parted lips and seeking tongues. His kiss was just like he was. Warm and solid and steady.

One wide palm slid into the waistband at the back of her pants, sliding down to cup her ass, rocking her hips into his. He growled out a groan against her lips. "What do you want from me, Clara?"

Her fingers froze where they were exploring the dips and grooves of his chest and stomach. "I don't—"

"Not the question I'm asking right now, Darlin'." His head lifted just enough his eyes could meet hers. "Right here. Right now. What do you want from me?"

The answer was still the same. "I don't know."

"I think you do." He ran his nose alongside hers. "I think you just don't want to admit it."

There was a lot she didn't want to admit to Brody. "I really don't know."

"That's a problem then." His hand slid up her back, easing free of her pajama pants. "Because nothing happens unless you know it's what you want to have happen."

There'd been more than a few times she'd wanted to scream at Brody since coming to Red Cedar Ranch. This was going on the list. "Are you serious?"

"As a heart attack." His lips lifted in a slow, shit-eating

grin. "For now you've gotta make it real clear we're on the same page."

"What page are you on?"

The grin on his face changed. The blue eyes holding hers darkened as Brody leaned into her. "I'm on the page where I get to listen to you come in my horse barn with my hand between your legs," his eyes dipped to where her shirt was still shoved up between them, "and my mouth—"

Her knees gave out, forcing her to hold onto him as she sagged against him.

At nothing more than a pretty basic description of one of a million fantasies she'd had about him.

Million might have been a low estimate.

"What's wrong, Clara?" The low rumble of his voice made everything that much worse. "Not used to a man telling you what he plans to do to you?"

Definitely not. "It's probably a stroke."

"Then you might want to get checked before I start telling you what else I plan to do with my mouth." His lips were right against her ear. "But that'll have to wait until I can convince you to find your way into my bed. I want you naked the first time I taste your—"

"Stop." She squeezed her eyes closed, trying to block out the images Brody's words conjured up in her mind. "I can't think about that."

"You can." He nipped at her skin. "You probably should so you'll be ready." His mouth trailed down her neck. "But right now I need to know if I'm sending you back to bed relaxed and satisfied." His mouth caught her nipple, tugging it between his lips for a second before setting it free. "Or if I'm sending you to bed aching."

He made it seem like a simple decision. One she shouldn't be struggling with as much as she was.

But there was no going back after this.

Then again, there might already be no going back.

"It's just a touch, Clara." Brody's eyes came to hers. "That's all."

He'd already touched her. She's already touched him. What was a little more?

"Just a touch." Her fingers found the skin of his stomach, sliding over it. "That's all."

"That's right. Just a touch." He inhaled against her neck. "Can I touch you, Clara?"

Her eyes fell closed again. "Yes."

She expected him to immediately take what she'd given.

But he didn't.

Brody's hands went to her hips before sliding back to cup her ass, palming the fullness there before sliding up her back, one hand wrapping around the back of her neck as the other held her close, his mouth claiming hers in a kiss that was as consuming as everything else about him.

His smell. His taste. His words.

All of it sucked her in and dragged her down, threatening to drown her in waters she didn't know existed.

And it wasn't as upsetting as it should be.

It felt like forever before the hand at her lower back shifted, pressing lower, sliding skin over skin, into the fabric of her pants. Easing over the curve of her hip, following the line of her upper thigh down to the part of her he described perfectly.

Aching.

She ached. Just like he said.

The tips of his fingers brushed over her with a careful touch as his mouth dragged free of hers, the press of his other hand between her shoulders staying firm. The touch between her thighs pressed deeper, sliding between the lips of her pussy to immediately find the tiny spot begging for his attention, gliding over it a few times before pushing farther, sliding into her body. Brody groaned against her breast. "Damn it." He sucked her nipple deep as his fingers moved in time with the pull of his mouth.

When the pad of his thumb settled against her clit it was more than she could handle, the steady rhythm of his movements sending her over the edge almost immediately, forcing her hands to grip any part of him she could in an attempt to keep her body upright.

"I won't let you fall, Darlin'." His arm at her back pulled tighter. "Promise."

Her vision was blurry as she stared up at the barn ceiling, her head propped against the wood boards at her back. "Who is that coordinated?"

Brody's chuckle was low and deep in her ear. "I'm used to doing a few things at once." His hand slid free of her pants, adjusting the waistband as he did before pulling her shirt into place.

A yawn jumped free.

"I like the sound of that." Brody's weight shifted as he pulled her away from the wall. "Let's get you in bed."

Clara blinked, her vision still a little clouded. "But what about you?" The thin fabric of the athletic pants he wore did nothing to hide the fact that one of them was still going to bed with an ache.

"It's part of being a man, "Darlin'." He pulled her in for a quick kiss. "Sometimes you've gotta suffer for the greater good."

"What's the greater good in this scenario?"

His smile was almost devilish. "Convincing you to jump into this with both feet."

———

"WHERE MY BREAKFAST?" Michaela stood at the empty kitchen table, both hands flung out at her sides as she stared Clara's way.

"Breakfast doesn't last all day, Chickadee." Clara smiled as she went to the fridge. "You want some cheese?"

"I want mine eggs." Michaela's voice raised an octave, making it clear she was working her way toward the second melt-down of the day.

"Eggs are gone." Clara pulled out a red wax-covered cheese wheel. "If you're hungry you can have cheese, otherwise you have to wait until lunch."

"I want Mimi." The little girl's voice screeched through the kitchen as she started to wail.

"Mimi is at the inn working." Clara kept her voice calm and even as she went to crouch beside Michaela. "Would you like cheese, or do you want to wait until lunch?"

"I want Mimi." Giant tears ran down the toddler's face, along with a thin line of snot that dribbled from her nose.

Clara leaned to snag a tissue from one of the many boxes scattered around the house for this exact reason. "Mimi won't give you eggs either. Breakfast is done. We've talked about this." Michaela was beginning to get into the habit of throwing a fit during a meal then wanting to come back later and eat what she refused earlier, and with a whole herd of cowhands to feed it was simply not possible to bend to the toddler's temperaments. "You may have cheese, but that's all." Making the little girl go hungry wasn't anything she wanted to do, but the outbursts were happening more and more often and they were getting progressively louder and it was taking Michaela longer to calm down after each one.

It was time to nip this in the bud.

"I want eggies." Michaela's head dropped back as her wailing escalated.

Clara calmly shook her head. "No eggs until breakfast tomorrow." She held the cheese out. "You may have cheese."

Michaela immediately fell to the ground, crumpling to a flailing pile of enraged blonde curls and crocodile tears.

Clara stood, walking to one of the two dishwashers in the giant kitchen and went back to unloading it, ignoring the child rolling across the floor, screaming like she was in the middle of an exorcism.

By the time the plates and cups were all stashed away, Michaela's cries had all but stopped. As Clara pulled out the bag of apples she offered to slice for lunch, Michaela finally pushed up from the floor, wiping one arm across her running nose. She came to stand beside where Clara was working. "I can has cheese?"

"Of course." Clara pulled the wax away and held the circle out.

"Fanks." Michaela took the white wheel and turned to go watch the last of the show the girls watched between breakfast and lunch.

Clara smiled as the little girl disappeared into the front of the house. She grabbed an apple and went to work chopping it up. It was barely in fourths before a solid press of warmth against her back nearly made her chop off one of her fingers.

"Careful." Brody reached around the blade of her knife to snag a slice.

"You scared me." She peeked over her shoulder at him. "And you be careful. Anyone could walk in."

"Not true." His head came to rest in the crook of her neck. "Everyone is working."

"Isn't that what you should be doing?"

"I'm the boss. I get to do what I want." One arm came to band around her waist as he bit into the chunk of apple he stole. "How's Michaela doing?"

"I'm pretty sure she hates me a little." It was difficult to be strong in the face of big blue eyes filled with tears, but it would be worth it.

"I can guarantee you she doesn't hate you." Brody popped the last of the apple into his mouth before wrapping his other arm in line with the first. "Whose bed does she find her way into every morning?"

"The gate slows them down a little." After Brody discovered the girls were sneaking into her room every morning he tried to figure out a way to stop them, but his daughters were having none of it.

"I'll figure something out."

"It's fine. They really don't bother me." If nothing else it was nice to know both girls still wanted to be around her even though she was upsetting their whole routine with letter practicing and counting.

And no more day-long breakfasts.

"I'm not worried about you." His body pressed tighter to her back as his lips ran along her bare shoulder. "I plan on having you in my bed and I don't enjoy little girl elbows jabbed into my ribs."

Clara stared down at the apple she was cutting with eyes so wide they burned. "I'm not so sure waking up in your bed is a good idea."

"So it's just the waking up there part you have an issue with?" His voice was low in her ear. "I can work with that for now."

The weight of his body disappeared.

Clara turned just as he walked out the door.

Did she just agree to being in his bed as long as she wasn't there in the morning?

"Cla-la? I can has some cheese too?"

Clara plastered on a smile as panic worked its way up her spine. "Yes, you can have some cheese." She grabbed a stick from the fridge for Leah, opening it and passing it over. "Are you ready for story time?"

She'd been working hard to establish a routine for the girls. Everyone else on the ranch had one, it would be easier if they did too.

But right now all she wanted to do was sit and stare at a wall, trying to figure out how to finagle her way out of ending up in Brody's bed.

Not that she didn't want to be there.

But there were people besides them in the house, namely Maryann and Bill. How would it look if one of them saw her sneaking away from Brody's room at night?

It would look like she was sexing him, which is exactly what she'd be doing.

"Cla-la?" Leah stared up at her, open-mouth chewing the cheese stick she ate like the savage she was, biting off chunks instead of peeling it down. "I can pick the story?"

"Today it's your turn to pick the story." She gave Leah a smile. "You go and get the book you want and I'll be there in just a second."

Leah gave her a toothy, cheese-filled grin. "Kay."

Clara hacked through the last two apples before putting the lid on the container and sliding it into the fridge, blowing out a breath as she turned toward the living room.

It would all be fine.

As long as she could stay the hell out of Brody Pace's bedroom.

CHAPTER TWELVE

"IT'S NICE OUT here." Clara gave Brody a little smile from the saddle she put on Edgar all by herself.

"It is." He managed to lure her out after dinner, stealing her away while his parents played a board game with the kids.

His mother was wise to his intentions, but at least she was keeping quiet about it.

For now.

One wrong move though, and she wouldn't hesitate to put him in his place.

And that place would be as far removed from Clara as she could get him. "I think you're making some headway with Michaela."

Clara rolled her eyes his way. "I don't know about that."

"She only screamed for fifteen minutes at dinner. That's ten minutes less than normal."

Clara smiled as she looked out over the fields. "She's headstrong."

"Like someone else I know."

Her attention came his way. "I'm not sure whether to be flattered or offended."

"Definitely flattered." He egged Elvis on, urging the horse closer to Edgar. "Means you aren't afraid to go after what you want."

Clara's smile slipped. "I'm not sure that's true."

He reached over to grab her hand, kicking himself for teaching her to ride on her own. Right now she could be in front of him. Close enough he could hold her tight.

Among other things.

Brody stroked his thumb across the back of her hand. "I want to show you something."

"Do we get to ride fast?" Her smile was back and her eyes were shining.

She loved it almost as much as Edgar did. It was the one problem his mother had with the gelding.

His need for speed.

Edgar was gentle and a lover of a horse, but he took every opportunity to run you gave him, always pushing it a little farther than his mother wanted to go.

Clara was a different story.

She loved the race as much as Edgar did. They were two peas in a pod, their dark hair flying in the wind as they raced across the ground.

"We can go fast whenever you want." He shot her a wink. "I'm always happy to go fast."

Seeing her with Michaela today solidified what he already knew.

Clara was right.

She fit in at Red Cedar Ranch. She fit into his family, settling into a spot that only she could fill.

And she fit him.

Clara was soft and sweet with a quiet strength she might not even realize she possessed.

But he knew.

And that's why they were coming out here today. So she could have another of the little escapes she deserved.

Clara barely nudged Edgar and he was already off, building speed as she settled into the rhythm of his steps. The woman was a natural rider.

Brody hung back, watching her ride ahead of him. It was the time Clara looked the lightest. The most free of the worries that bogged her down.

Tonight was about clearing up some of that fog. Finding another outlet for her to use.

Brody directed Elvis toward the most secluded part of the ranch. The section where the elevation started to increase, hinting at the mountains in the distance. Edgar followed suit, carrying Clara to the surprise Brody had for her.

After a few minutes of riding hard, Brody slowed Elvis. Edgar continued on a few more paces before his run slowed to a trot and then to a walk. Clara turned toward him. "Where are we going?"

Brody pointed toward the softly rolling land in front of them. "Here."

She rocked a little as Edgar walked toward the space. "I can't believe you own all this."

"You've only seen a tiny bit of it, Darlin." He eased Elvis in beside Edgar. "You've got a lot more rides before you see it all."

She smiled. "Good."

"No one really ever comes out here."

Clara peeked down at the ground. "There's not much grass."

"That's right." He reached out to smooth down Elvis' neck. "Almost not worth bringing the cattle all the way out here for it."

"So what do you use it for?"

"Right now, nothing." The space was the spot they escaped to as kids. Went when life was shit as adults. "I came here a lot after Ashley died."

Clara's eyes came his way, her expression soft. "I can't imagine what it was like to be alone with two babies."

"I think that might have made it easier. I had to go on. Had to move forward." Juggling two infants kept him from thinking about all he'd lost.

Most of the time. When it didn't, this was the place he went. Just to sit in the silence. "Some days it still got to me. That's when I came out here." Brody looked out over the space he once knew like the back of his hand. "I haven't been here in almost a year, though."

Clara was quiet. "Is that why you brought me here? So I could have a place to escape to when things get to me?"

"No." Brody dropped down to the ground and walked to Edgar's side, reaching one hand up her way. "Come on."

Clara's lips twisted into a little smile. "Watch your nuts."

He was still laughing when she dropped to the ground beside him. "I think this spot might already be rubbing off on you."

Clara leaned close to Edgar, giving him a stroke. "How's that?"

"There's no little ears out here to hear every word that comes out of your mouth."

Her eyes slowly came his way, lingering for a second. "I have a confession to make."

"Only one?" He backed away. "I feel like your life's been more exciting than that."

"You'd be surprised." Clara followed him as he walked backward toward a certain spot.

The fact that she went along with him settled comfortably in his gut. "What's your confession?"

Her full lips hinted at a smile. "You might think differently of me after I tell you."

"I bet you're wrong." There wasn't much of anything that could make him think differently of her. Clara was all he wouldn't have believed she'd be. "Tell me."

The smile she tried to hide snuck free. "I like to cuss."

"I might have already guessed that." It was plain as day that every shoot and darn that came out of her mouth was unsatisfying as hell. "And you're in the right place. Cowboy's aren't known for carrying on G-rated conversations."

"I heard." She peeked his way as she reached his side. "Your mom's still mad at Wayne."

"They're going to learn it eventually." Brody found her hand, wrapping it in his. "You ready?"

Clara's dark eyes widened. "For what?"

"Hollerin'." He tipped his head in the direction of the mountains barely visible in the distance. "Try it out."

Clara's expression was soft as her eyes stayed on him. "I don't really think I need to right now."

Well damn.

Brody brought her here, thinking he could give her something special. Something that couldn't be bought. Something that proved he saw her for what she was.

And instead he was the one getting a gift he didn't see coming.

"Good." Brody pulled Clara close, not quite ready to take her back to the house. He had to share her there. Walk a fine line to keep her comfortable with the way things were going.

Because everyone knew things were going. There was no hiding it. Not from anyone at the ranch.

But Clara didn't have to know that just yet.

He buried his nose in her hair, breathing deep. She smelled soft and sweet, just like always.

But also something else.

The scent of fresh air clung to every bit of her. "Do you like it here, Darlin'?"

Clara's arms laced around his neck as she curved against him. "I do."

He might not have given her what he planned, but hopefully there was something else Clara was finding with him.

Freedom.

"Your mom made pie."

"Are you really saying you'd rather go back and eat pie than be here with me?" He couldn't even make himself sound put out.

Clara leaned back, her eyes wide. "It's peach."

Brody's head fell back as he laughed. Something he wasn't accustomed to doing in this particular spot. "So I rank right under peach pie."

"Well." Her brows lifted a little. "Maybe not *right* under."

"Ouch."

"Have you not ever had ice cream?" Clara laughed as he squeezed her tighter.

"It's fine. As long as I'm there somewhere."

She stilled, her expression turning a little more serious. "You're there." She sighed. "Not that you should be."

"I definitely should be." He reached up to stroke across her cheek.

Her eyes followed the path of his hand. "Why do you always do that?"

Brody dragged his thumb across the softness of her skin. "You really want to know?"

"Now I'm not sure."

He chuckled. "It's where the horses like to be scratched."

"So you're petting me like a horse."

"I would think if anyone would like that it'd be you."

Clara's mouth slid into a little smile. "You're not wrong."

Brody brushed his lips over hers, giving himself just a little of what he craved before tugging her toward the horses. "Well if you're not going to let me hear you holler then let's go get some pie."

―――

"WHAT DO YOU have planned for the week, Dear?" Maryann snagged Clara's empty pie plate as she worked to free Michaela from her booster.

"I need to go into town to get Wyatt enrolled in school." Her eyes skimmed to Brody, hanging for just a second before pulling away. "And I need to do a little shopping."

"I'm free to watch the girls tomorrow if that's not too soon." Maryann rinsed the plates before loading them into the dishwasher.

"That would work actually." Clara turned to his mother. "Are you sure you don't mind?"

"Not at all, Dear." Maryann smiled wide at Clara. "I don't expect you to work around the clock. If you ever need time for yourself you just tell me. I'll make it work."

Clara's head dipped a little. "I just want to be sure Wyatt's set for school in the fall."

"That's because you're a good momma." His mother's eyes moved to him as Clara leaned to grab Leah from her seat. The sweet gaze she'd given Clara turned to a glare. "I want to be sure you are always happy here."

Instead of wiggling her way to the ground, Leah squirmed into Clara's lap, wide blue eyes staring up at the woman who might end up being more than any of them bargained for. "You happy Cla-la?"

Clara's smile was warm and soft. "I'm very happy."

Leah curled closer. "You can read me a story?"

"I can always read you a story." Clara stood up, hefting Leah with her as she went. "I think you might have worn yourself out today."

"I not tired."

"Of course not." Clara turned toward Brody. "Can you grab Michaela?"

"Yup." He jumped up from his seat, ready to get the hell away from his mother and the lecture she was dying to give him. He followed close behind as Clara passed through the hall toward the living room. She turned to him, her voice low.

"You owe me."

Brody leaned close to her ear. "I'm happy to pay that debt off anytime you want, Darlin'." Her eyes were still wide as they stepped into the family room where his father was sitting with Wyatt and Michaela, watching as Clara's son helped Michaela stack a random assortment of items into a tower. "It's bedtime, Little Monster."

Clara pointed to the scatter of toys across the area rug. "Pick up your toys."

"I not want to." Michaela stood. "Wyatt will do it."

"No." Clara passed Leah off to Brody as she went in to where Michaela was gearing up for another fit. "You helped make the mess. You must help clean it up." She dropped to her knees on the carpet. "Wyatt will help, but he wasn't the only one playing with the toys."

Michaela's face scrunched up.

"Tonight is your turn to choose the story, but you can't choose until you clean up your toys." Clara picked up a foam block and held it out for Michaela.

His daughter's cheeks pinked, flushing with the impending tantrum.

Brody took a step forward. "If you don't pick up your toys then you can't listen to Clara's story."

Michaela's little mouth dropped open.

He'd been bad for letting his daughters get away with just about anything. They were cute as hell.

And the only thing that brought him happiness for a long time.

But now he was facing the consequences of his actions in the form of a tiny tantrum factory.

"Go on." Brody used his free hand to point to the items at Michaela's feet. "Pick it up so we can go read a story."

Leah leaned back to peek up at him, her lids already drooping. "You gonna come too?"

"Might as well." He could feel Clara's eyes on him. "Seems like a pretty popular thing. I might come see what the fuss is all about."

A steady knocking sound came from the floor.

Michaela was kicking the pile of toys toward the bin. She silently picked them up and tossed them in before turning and marching to the stairs.

His dad chuckled from the recliner in the corner. "That one there does not like doing what she doesn't want to do." He shot Clara a grin. "Bout time she met someone more stubborn than she is."

Clara gave his dad a tight smile. "You ready for bed, Wy?"

Wyatt stood from his spot on the floor, going straight to Bill and giving him a hug. "Night."

The move didn't seem to come as a surprise to his dad. He patted Wyatt's back with one hand. "Sleep good so you can show your momma around town tomorrow."

Wyatt grinned. "Okay." He turned and raced up the stairs with Clara following behind him and Brody and Leah bringing up the rear.

By the time they got the girls' faces scrubbed and teeth brushed, they were both glassy-eyed and yawning. Michaela grabbed a book from Clara's nightstand as she struggled to climb onto the mattress. Brody boosted her up before stretching across the foot of the bed.

Leah settled in next to Michaela with Wyatt the last to climb in. Clara sat at the edge next to Wyatt and started the story.

It was a familiar book. One he'd heard read many times before.

He hadn't been able to bring himself to read it in the three years it sat on the shelf in the girls' room.

Now he was regretting that.

Because it was clear what was happening had little to do with the actual story.

All three sets of eyes were on Clara, watching her as she read to them in a soft, sweet voice about a group of animals getting ready for bed. Leah played with the sleeve of Wyatt's shirt as her breathing started to slow and her eyes started to droop. By the time the story was over both toddlers were asleep and Wyatt was well on his way.

Clara eased up from the bed and pulled back the covers so her little boy could get out. She dropped a kiss to his head as he passed on his way to bed. She watched him go, her eyes finding Brody when Wyatt was gone. "You wanna help me get these two in their beds?"

Brody stood up, a peace he hadn't known in years settling in his chest. "I don't think so, Darlin'."

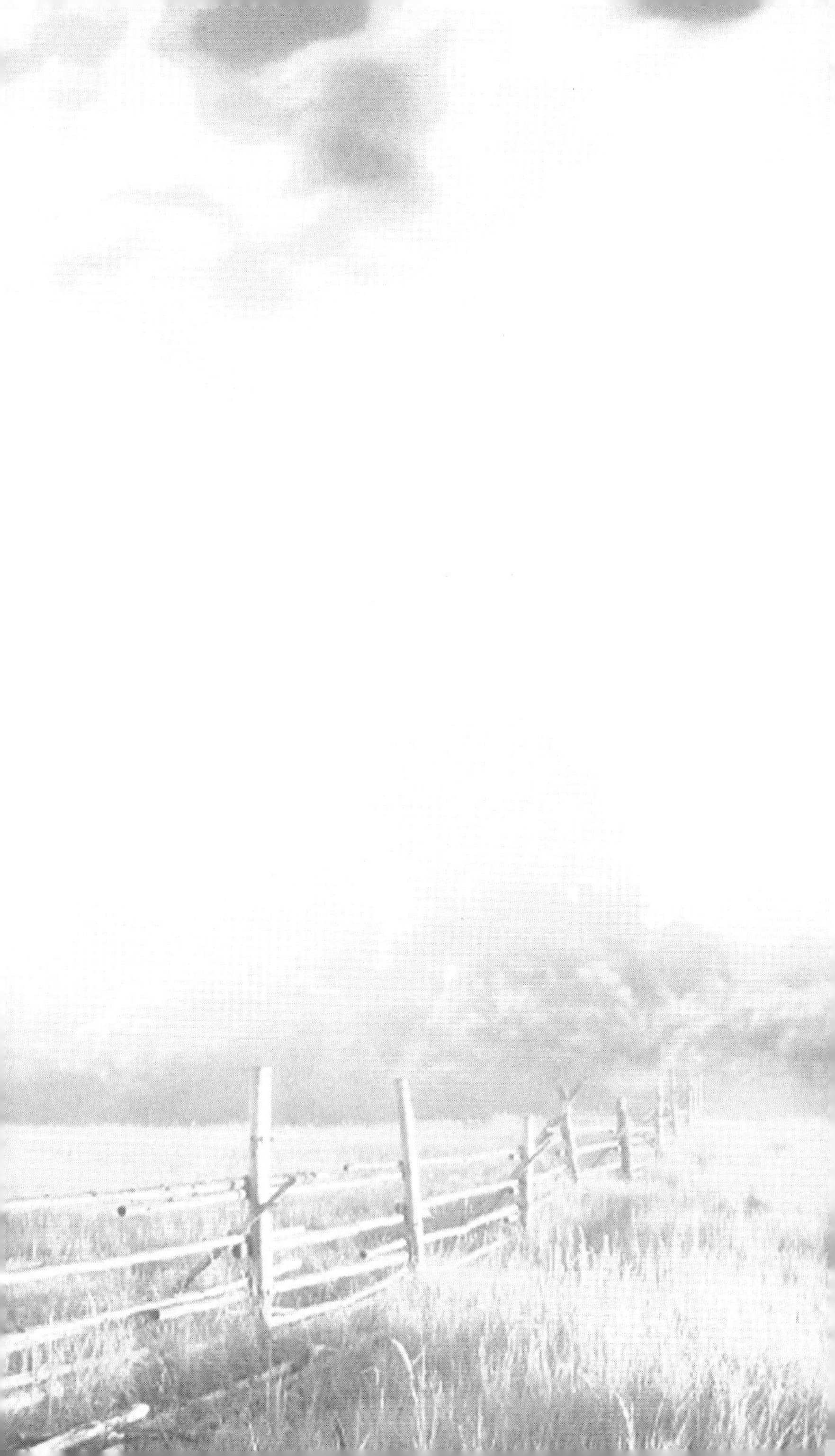

CHAPTER THIRTEEN

THERE WAS ONLY so much *fake it till you make it* to go around.

That meant she had to fall back on the other thing that got her through the past year.

Not thinking too hard.

It would be easy to talk herself out of this. Just like it would have been easy to decide going back to school would be impossible.

Moving to Montana would be crazy.

She could never ride a horse.

If she considered them too long, not a single one would have happened.

Clara took a step closer to Brody. "What *do* you think then?"

"You know what I think, Clara. I haven't tried to hide it from you."

No. He hadn't.

"What matters is what you think." Brody's blue gaze was

serious as it held hers. "And if you want me to haul two little girls to their beds I will do it with a smile on my face."

She turned to look back at where Michaela and Leah slept. "They do look comfortable, don't they?"

"They'll be fine either way. You're all I'm worried about right now."

Clara faced Brody. "You don't have to worry about me. I'm not a child."

"I will always worry about you, Clara. You can't stop that." He eased a little closer, but still didn't touch her. "You think a man doesn't worry about his wife's happiness?"

"I'm not your wife."

His lips twitched at the edges. "I'm very aware of that."

"And I can make decisions just fine." She lifted her chin a little. "I am completely capable of deciding what I want to do in my life."

"Happy to hear that." Brody inched in a bit more.

The best things that happened to her were things that she jumped into with both feet. Things that scared the shit out of her but she dove in anyway.

And Brody Pace fit the bill.

"I'm not staying in your bed until morning." She might be willing to take this chance, but dragging Wyatt or the girls into it wasn't going to happen.

"Anything else?"

That made her pause.

Should there be anything else? "No?"

Brody chuckled low in his chest. "Well if you think of anything, you be sure to let me know." He snagged her hand in his, pulling her toward the door.

"I haven't taken a shower." Clara resisted his pull. She hadn't had sex in more than a while, and the last thing she wanted was to be any more self-conscious than she was already going to be.

The man was physical perfection. Sex stacked between boots and a hat, with a deep drawl that might be able to finish her off all on its own.

"There's a bathroom connected to my room." Brody tugged her enough to get her feet moving. "I'd be happy to show it to you."

"How nice of you."

"Got nothing to do with being nice, Darlin'. More the opposite, actually." Brody led her down the hall, walking backwards as he continued to coax her along. "The shower is plenty big enough to fit two people."

"Interesting." It was the only word she could manage as images of Brody's naked, water-slicked body hijacked her mind.

"It is." He passed through the door to his room, closing the door behind her and twisting the small lock on the handle. "I've found it more interesting lately." Brody came close, slowly pressing her backward until her thighs bumped the bed, knocking her butt to the mattress. "Then again I've found a lot of things more interesting lately." He dropped to his knees in front of her and went to work untying the sneakers she wore, tossing each one away after he slipped them off.

"Like?"

"Like life in general." Brody tugged off her socks, sending them to the same pile with her shoes as his eyes came to hers. "I was lonely as hell before you came." He leaned close.

"I know it doesn't make sense with all the people around here."

Clara dropped her head closer to his. "I understand."

She'd been lonely for years.

Learned to live with it to the point that it was difficult to let anyone into the bubble she'd created. It was safer.

"I know you do.'" Brody's hands came to her face, one palm resting along each side of her jaw as his eyes held hers.

There was so much there. So much she still couldn't acknowledge.

Not yet.

Clara looped her arms around his neck, pressing her lips to his to avoid seeing what she wasn't ready to see.

Brody pulled her close, dragging her off the bed as he stood. Her toes skimmed across the wood floor as he all but carried her to the open door at one corner of the large room. He flipped on the light with one hand, stepping inside before kicking the door closed, his mouth holding hers the whole time with a kiss that stole her breath and muddled her mind.

All her rational thoughts about this situation centered on the fact that Brody would be seeing her naked.

All her fantasies though, revolved around what *she* would see and now that Clara was facing the prospect of a naked Brody Pace, there was a feeling of urgency.

Some might call it need.

She was sticking with urgency.

Clara grabbed the hem of the fitted shirt he tortured her with, grabbing it tight and wrestling it up his body.

Brody didn't make her fight with it long. His lips immediately pulled from hers and he shucked the thing in one easy move, tossing it away before coming right back.

His skin was warm. Almost hot as it pressed against the uncovered parts of her.

Not that there were many.

Clara grabbed her own shirt, pulling at it the same way she'd done his, trying to work it as far off as she could with his body pressed so close.

Before she could get loose, Brody wrapped one arm around her waist, moving her across the room to where the shower was. He leaned to reach in and switch the water on before turning back.

His mouth was right back on hers, as warm and solid as the arms holding her tight.

But she didn't want him to hold her tight.

Clara wrestled her hands between their bodies, her fingers digging at the waistband of his jeans, fighting the button free of its hole before working the zipper down.

She wanted him naked. Needed that to distract her from the fact that she would also soon be naked too.

Not that she was insecure about how she looked. Her body was perfectly normal and fine.

It was the thought of having nothing between them. Nothing keeping any part of her from any part of him.

Clara pushed at the worn pants, trying to shove them down. Before she could make any headway Brody stepped back. He kicked his boots off, eyes never leaving hers as he dropped what remained of his clothing to the bathroom floor.

She tried to keep her attention on his face.

But...

The temptation was too much.

Her gaze dropped all on its own.

"Holy shit." The words escaped with the rush of air from her lungs.

"Not gonna complain about that reaction." She could hear the smile in his words.

Didn't see it though.

Because there was so much else to look at.

Brody reached back, sticking one hand under the water before pulling the curtain to one side and stepping in. He gave her a wink before dragging the curtain back into place.

Cutting off her view.

That was mean.

Clara stood there for a second.

"The water's nice and warm, Darlin'."

The scent of fresh water and pine drifted along the humid air.

He was soaping up. Running his hands over—

She leaned a little to one side, trying to get a peek around the edge of the curtain.

No luck. If she wanted to see what was happening, there was only one choice.

She had to get in there with him.

Get naked without the distraction of his body to carry her along.

Fake it till she made it.

Clara wiggled out of her shirt and jeans, piling them up with Brody's. Her bra and panties were the last to go.

She took a deep breath and jumped, pulling back the curtain and stepping in behind him.

"I was startin' to think you changed your mind." He slowly turned to face her, the spray of water rinsing away the last of the suds on his skin.

Clara managed to shake her head a little.

It was difficult to do anything but stare. She'd never seen anything like him. Definitely not up close and personal.

Very personal.

Her eyes moved over his chest and across the stomach she loved to touch. They dipped lower, snagging on the line of his already-erect cock.

"Sorry about that." Brody shoved it down with one hand as he pulled her close, his body slick as it pressed against hers. "Ignore it."

That was not something she was remotely interested in ignoring.

She traced the tips of her fingers across the skin of his upper thighs, fully intending to go straight for what he told her to ignore.

Before she could make her way there, Brody pinned her to him and switched their places, the warm water immediately soaking her hair and back.

"I'm gonna be real honest with you right now, Darlin'." Brody grabbed a bottle of unscented body wash that looked to be exactly what she regularly used and squirted some into his palm. "I came into this with real high hopes." His eyes dragged down her body as he rubbed his hands together. "And it seems like I might have been a little optimistic."

She was trying to follow what he was saying, but there were only so many cells in her brain, and most of them were currently occupied by the body in front of her. "Uh-huh."

"I was expecting you to look," his soapy palms came to her shoulders, working over her skin as they slid down her arm, "good." He said the last word slower than the ones before it. "Just not this good." His hands moved back up her arms, working over her neck with a gentle touch before gliding down her front, curving over her breasts as his thumbs stroked across each nipple simultaneously, bringing them to stiff peaks almost immediately.

Brody groaned, his dark gaze snagging where his hands lingered. "Damn it." His touch slid away as he worked the suds lower, over her belly and hips before one hand worked between her thighs, keeping the soap only in the places it belonged before once again pulling away.

He pressed his body to hers, pushing her farther under the water. "Tip your head back."

Clara's eyes closed as his hands came to ease her head into the stream, strong fingers working through her hair.

His touch disappeared for a minute before coming back. A familiar scent filled the shower. Clara opened an eye to peek at him. "That's my shampoo."

"Not technically." Brody's fingers massaged her scalp as he washed her hair.

She glanced at the line of familiar bottles along the ledge. "I might have checked to see what you use."

"So your plan was always to lure me into your shower." She wasn't hating it if it was.

"Among other things." Brody tipped her head back, rinsing out the shampoo before working a little conditioner through her ends.

"I'm impressed with your shampoo skills." All the tension she brought into the bathroom was gone, worked away by Brody's strong hands and the heat of the water.

"I've had a fair bit of practice." Brody reached behind her to switch off the water. "I figured I should use it to my advantage." He snagged a towel from a hook just outside, bringing it into the warm cocoon of the shower and wrapping it around her before pulling the curtain open and stepping out, his naked body still soaking wet.

He held her hand as she stepped out beside him onto the plush mat. Once she was out Brody grabbed the other towel and draped it over her head, carefully squeezing the water from her hair.

It was the most attention a man had ever paid to her.

The most care she'd ever been shown by anyone.

"Thank you."

Brody's eyes came to hers. "For?"

She shrugged. There was no way to explain what she was appreciative for. It probably wouldn't make sense to him even if she tried.

His lips lifted in a barely-there smile as he took the towel from her hair and wrapped it around his waist. "Come on."

It didn't take anything more than those two words for her to follow him, eyes on his as Brody backed into his room, leading her toward the bed.

He stopped, reaching for her hand. She ignored it, finished the last few steps all on her own.

Clara rested her hands against his chest. His skin was still damp and warm from the shower. "You didn't dry off."

Before she could overthink, Clara pulled the tuck of her towel loose, letting it fall free. She lifted the soft terry to his skin, using it to wipe away the moisture still clinging there.

Once his chest and arms were done she lifted her eyes to his. "Turn around."

Brody did as she asked without a word, turning so she could run the towel down the wide expanse of his back and shoulders.

"Okay."

She held her breath as he turned back to face her. As their eyes met Clara let the towel in her hand drop to the floor.

"You're killing me a little, you know that, Darlin'?"

"I don't mean to." It wasn't exactly an apology.

"That's probably the only thing that might save me." Brody's eyes dragged down her body. "Because if you were trying, I might be as good as useless."

"Useless doesn't sound very good."

"It's not." He eased closer, pulling her tight to him as he turned, putting the bed right behind her. "So let's make a deal that you keep not meaning to." He lifted her up, one of his knees coming to press into the mattress as he leaned forward. "At least for now."

"That doesn't sound very good either." Clara laced one arm around his neck as Brody lowered her to the mattress, as soon as her back rested against the soft sheets she reached for him with her free hand, sliding it down the center of his chest.

He didn't seem to notice until her fingers tangled in the towel still tied around his waist.

Brody caught her wandering hand by the wrist, pulling it away. "I thought we had a deal?"

"I don't remember making any deals." She went for him with her other hand, scoffing when he immediately caught that one too.

Brody brought her hands together, holding them with one of his and pressing them to the pillows above her head. "You should make the deal. It's in your best interest." He leaned in close, running his lips along the curve of her shoulder.

"But I want to touch you."

Brody groaned against her skin, his free hand moving down the line of her body. "Darlin', if I can't even handle hearing you say it, I sure as hell won't be able to handle you actually doing it."

"That's not fair." Clara wiggled around. "You can touch me but I can't touch you?"

"Seems like." His mouth dipped lower, nipped at the swell of her breast. He reached between them to tug the towel free of his body, tossing it away. "Unless you want to watch me make a fool of myself." The length of his frame pressed into hers. "Because I can promise you that's what will happen."

Clara wiggled her hands, trying to twist free of his hold, working her body as she did, hoping to get a little extra leverage. Her belly rubbed against his straining length, dragging another groan from his throat.

Brody's free hand pinned her hip in place. "Damn it." His whole body shifted.

His hand dropped hers.

For a second she was excited to finally be free to do all the things she'd imagined.

Touch him.

Taste him.

But Brody was pulling away from her reach.

She started to sit up. "Where are you going?"

Brody's eyes lifted to hers, a wicked glint catching in the light.

As his mouth lowered.

"Damn it, Brod—" The rest of his name was cut off on a

gasp as his lips met her skin, immediately focusing on the one thing he had to know would bring her down.

He wasn't wrong.

Clara dropped back to the mattress as his tongue flicked against her, rolling her eyes closed.

His hands gripped her thighs, spreading them wider as his shoulders worked between them, the constant stroke of his tongue never once losing its pace.

Reality was never like fantasy could be. Reality was full of fears and insecurities and the truth.

It never lived up to expectations built on fantasy.

But Brody Pace was making a habit of proving her wrong.

It was another problem for another day.

Because right now all she could think about was this particular wrong he was proving.

He hooked his hands around her legs, pulling her down the mattress and tight against his mouth, groaning as his tongue again found the spot that could undo her in seconds.

Who was making a fool of themselves now?

"Brody stop." She reached for him, grabbing at the only thing she could. Her fingers laced into his dark hair, pulling the damp strands tight as she tried to break the contact threatening to send her over the edge before they'd even really started. "Please."

"No." The word was a sharp growl against her flesh as he held her tighter, pinning her in place, refusing her desperate pleas for mercy. His lips wrapped around the spot he owned, sucking with the same rhythm his tongue set.

The room went black and silent, everything falling away as her body pulled tight. There was nothing else.

Just him and that damn spot he refused to leave alone for even a second.

She broke apart on a cry and a curse, the hands that once shoved at him holding Brody in place as he dragged more from her than she knew she had to give.

Clara blinked up at the ceiling.

Brody's wide warm body worked its way up hers, wicked lips leaving a path of heat as they blazed a trail over her belly and ribs.

She thought she was numb. Thought he'd shorted out every nerve in her body with that one single spot.

But as those damn wicked lips closed around her nipple it became clear the only thing that he'd shorted out was her brain. Her back arched, pressing her deeper into his mouth as it pulled at her in long draws, each one seeming like it tightened a string connected to the ache between her legs.

An ache that shouldn't still be there.

And yet it was.

Dark and needy and almost painful.

"Brody, please." Her last please was for mercy.

This was the same.

His body leaned away for a second, the loss of his mouth and his touch leaving her feeling desperate.

Clara grabbed for him, trying to drag Brody back.

"We've established you're not ready for all I am, Darlin'." A sharp tearing sound pierced the haze around her. "That means you've gotta be patient for just a second."

Her gaze dragged down to where his hand worked down the length of his cock, securing the only thing that would be between them tonight.

He settled over her, the broad head of him pressing just

against the center of her. The heat of his stare pulling her eyes to his as one hand came to her face, thumb stroking over her cheek.

Brody didn't move as his eyes searched hers.

"Please." It wasn't for mercy this time. This time the please was half permission, half prayer.

One for him. One for her.

His forehead dropped to hers as his hips slowly pressed forward, working the length of him into the tight fit of her.

Clara couldn't look away from his face. The lines of focus between his brows. The clench of his jaw. The dark blue depths of the eyes refusing to let hers go.

The air rushed from his chest as his body met hers, fully joined.

His was the only breath taken as Brody immediately pulled back, nearly free, before pushing back, filling her again.

And again.

It was impossible to think about the breathing she'd struggled with for so long.

Air was no longer as important as it once seemed.

All that mattered was him.

There.

With her.

Her hands went to the face still so close to hers, holding it the way his eyes held hers. Gripping the connection between them as if it might slip away at any second.

The ache he created bloomed, growing to something else entirely. A throb. All heat. All need.

"Brody."

"That's right, Darlin'." He shifted, the tight line of his

stomach pressing against her, rubbing as his hips continued to work. "Give me what I want."

He could take it.

She knew it.

He knew it.

"Yes." She shoved her hands back, fingers stabbing into his hair, holding him tight.

"Now, Clara. Give it to me now." His movements were faster, almost frenzied. Urgency had his voice tight, his teeth clenched.

"Please." A plea.

Not hers.

His.

"Yes." It was short and nearly silent. All her lungs could propel as she fell apart for the second time.

Brody's eyes shut tight as he jerked against her in quick, deep thrusts. His head dropped to the pillow beside hers, the ragged saw of his breath warming her ear.

His weight grounded her. His warmth was a blanket between her and everything waiting.

The worry.

The fear.

The uncertainty.

Brody kept it all away.

Or made none of it matter.

CHAPTER FOURTEEN

"WHAT DO YOU think of your new school?" Clara walked beside Wyatt as they headed down the street toward the small downtown area of Moss Creek.

"It's kinda small." Wyatt glanced down as Leah tucked her hand into his. "But that's okay."

"You goin' to school, Wy-it?" Leah jumped twice in a row, landing on both feet each time.

"At the end of summer." Wyatt held Leah's hand tight as she continued to dance around.

"I can go to school too?" Michaela's little voice pulled Brody's attention to where she walked at his side.

But Michaela wasn't asking him.

"Not yet." Clara gave her a smile. "But maybe next year."

Michaela's lips pressed into a frown.

"Are you hungry?" Clara quickly moved the conversation along, managing to distract Michaela from the fit she was contemplating.

"Yup." Michaela swung her hand where it held Clara's. "I will have... um..."

"Grilled cheese?" Brody stopped, grabbing the door to The Wooden Spoon and pulling it open. "Miss Mae makes a darn good grilled cheese."

Wyatt walked in first, taking Leah toward a booth in the far corner of the best place to eat in town. Clara lifted her brows as she passed him. Her mouth pulled into a smile. "This place is really nice."

"Don't sound so surprised." He followed close behind her, pressing one hand to the small of her back as every eye in the place came their way.

It wasn't every day someone new came to Moss Creek, and he wanted to be sure there were no misunderstandings about Clara and her availability.

"Brody Pace." Mae Wells' voice carried in through the kitchen service window.

A second later the swinging door separating the dining room from the kitchen bumped open and she breezed through, her blonde hair wound into a thick braid down the back of her head. "I don't get to see your face in town much."

"The ranch keeps me busy." He leaned in as Mae caught him in a friendly hug. "Plus taking care of these two Monsters."

"They are angels." Mae shoved him aside, her eyes locked on Clara. "And you must be Clara."

Clara's smile froze on her face. "Yeah."

Mae lifted her brows as she leaned closer to Clara, lowering her voice. "You have quite the fan club around here."

Clara relaxed just a little, her gaze moving to where Michaela was climbing up into the booth where Wyatt and Leah sat. "They only like me because I feed them."

"I wasn't talking about the girls." Mae's smile turned devilish. "I was referring to all the ranch hands." She shot Brody a wink. "Go sit down. I'll be over in a minute."

Damn Mae. She knew that would stick in his ribs and she loved it.

Because the woman took any opportunity to punish the Pace boys for what one of them did.

All for one and one for all at its finest.

Brody led Clara to the table, catching any eye he could that came her way. Word traveled fast around here, and it was about time he could use that to his advantage.

Wyatt and both girls were sitting across one side of the booth with Wyatt in the middle. Clara slid into the other bench seat and Brody moved in beside her, scooting close and dropping his arm along the back of the seat, letting his thumb brush her skin. It was something none of the kids could see.

But every other eye in the place could.

"How are you ladies today?" Mae was back with a stack of menus. She set one in front of Wyatt before passing the next to Clara.

"Do you has brownies today?" Michaela was Mae's biggest fan.

Mostly because Mae made the best brownies in Montana.

"I think that depends on how well you eat your lunch." Mae's smile was warm as she crouched down close at Michaela's side. "I have something I think you will really like for lunch. Can I surprise you with it?"

Leah leaned around Wyatt toward Mae. "Can I has a surprise too?"

"Of course." Mae's smile went to Wyatt next. "What about you, handsome?"

"Lunch surprise." He grinned at Mae.

Looked like Mae Wells' fan club included more than just his mother and Michaela.

"Make it four." Clara stacked her menu onto his.

Brody picked up the stack and held them Mae's way. "I'll keep it easy for you then and say five lunch surprises."

"Not used to men making my life easy." Mae grabbed the menus and headed back to the kitchen, disappearing through the door.

Clara opened the boxes of crayons Mae set down in front of each of the girls, passing out the cheap wax sticks as she worried her lower lip between her teeth.

Wyatt took turns helping the girls find words in the searches printed on the paper activity mats in front of them.

Clara moved from chewing her lip to tying the paper from her straw into knots.

Brody leaned into her ear. "What's wrong, Darlin'?"

She shook her head just a little. "Nothing." Clara scooted closer, bumping him with her body. "I need to use the bathroom."

Brody eased out of the booth. "It's in the back corner."

"Thank you." Clara didn't look his way as she passed, her eyes instead moving around the dining room. She hustled away, making a beeline for the hall leading to the bathrooms.

Brody sat back down, turning to shoot a look around the space. A table of ranch hands from Cross Creek sat at the far end of the room.

Not a single one of them looked his way.

Brody turned back to the kids sitting across from him. Wyatt stared at him across the table.

"What's wrong, Little Man?"

Wyatt shook his head.

"Seems like something's wrong."

Wyatt's eyes dropped to the table between them. "I'm just a little nervous about school."

"Makes sense." He'd never been a new kid, but could imagine what it might be like.

"It does?"

"Sure. Change is scary." Brody collected the bits of straw wrapper scattered around from Clara's knot tying. "Maybe I can take you and introduce you to some of the kids before school starts."

"We could do that?"

"Of course."

"How do you know who will be in my class?"

It was an innocent question that showed just how different this life was from what Wyatt was used to. "I know just about everyone around here."

Wyatt's eyes widened. "Really?"

Brody tipped his head in a nod. "Really."

One of the Smith sisters had a son who had to be almost Wyatt's age. Maybe he could have his mother invite them to the ranch for a visit.

"No thank you." Clara's voice was stronger than he'd ever heard it as it carried in from the back hall.

A low murmur followed just after the solid rejection.

Brody was up out of his seat before the man's voice finished the last words it would say with all the teeth God gave him.

He rounded the corner, catching sight of Clara immediately. She was backed into a corner by an unfamiliar man.

But Clara looked anything but cornered.

She stood tall, her chin lifted, eyes narrowed as she stared down the ranch hand spending his last moments in Moss Creek. "I said no. Don't expect me to say it again."

"Come on, sweetheart. What do you expect me to think comin' in here all cuddled up with your boss?" The man moved closer. "I think you're more friendly than you want to admit."

Clara's head slowly tipped to one side as one of her eyes got a little more squinty than the other. "I think you better go find your friends before—"

"Before what?" Another step closer. "Before Brody starts asking questions about where the nanny he's fucking disappeared to?"

Brody grabbed the hand by the back of his neck, twisting him to one side and shoving hard, smashing the asshole's face into the wall. He kept his grip and immediately yanked the man back, dragging him down the hall and toward the front of the restaurant. He used his free hand to grip the waistband of the hand's jeans, hefting him across the table where the rest of his buddies sat, knocking plates of food and glasses of water across the floor.

"He broke my nose." The man who should have known the risk he was taking grabbed his bleeding nose with one hand.

Brody looked to the hand who'd been at Cross Creek the longest. "Get him out of here."

"What in the hell happened?" Ben stood, his eyes

immediately finding Clara. "Goddammit, Duke." He grabbed the injured man by the shoulder and shoved him toward the door. "What in the hell is wrong with you?"

The rest of the men at the table looked at each other.

Ben turned to them. "Don't just sit there. Get up. We're leaving."

Brody stood and watched as the hands stood, one by one, and filed out the door, Ben dragging Duke along as they went.

"Brody Pace!"

He turned to find not one, but two women glaring his way.

Mae had a plate balanced on each hand. "I hope you know you're the one's gonna clean that mess up."

―――

"WHERE'S CLARA?"

His mother turned his way. "Why should I tell you?"

"Why shouldn't you tell me?" He'd been trying to find her since dinner ended, coming up empty in all the normal places. She wasn't with the girls. She wasn't with Wyatt.

And she wasn't in the barn.

"Seems like I might have a few reasons not to tell you." His mother wiped her hands on the towel slung over one shoulder. "Maybe Clara needs a break."

"That's what I'm trying to give her." He wanted to take her out for a ride. Show her more of the ranch.

Have her to himself after the shitty day he'd had.

"Maybe she needs a break from *you*." Maryann glared his way. "Just let her be."

He didn't want to let her be.

He wanted to make sure she was okay after what happened at Mae's today. "I want to talk to her."

"What part of *leave her be* don't you understand?" His mother shook her head. "I swear, sometimes I wonder how you got so thick-headed."

Brody huffed out a breath.

"Don't you huff at me." His mother grabbed the towel from her shoulder and swung it straight at his face, slapping the damp fabric across his cheek. "Because of you I've got to help Liza Cross find another hand for her ranch."

"Because of me?" Brody's lingering anger flared to life immediately. "Do you even know what he said to her?"

"All I know is you had one hell of an expensive lunch that you're going to be paying for in more than just cash."

"What's that supposed to mean?"

His mother smirked at him. "It means just because a woman is quiet, doesn't mean she can't hold her own."

"No one said she coul—"

He knew where Clara was.

Brody turned, walking out the back door as his mother continued hollering. "Brody Pace, you leave that girl alone."

He scanned the pasture connected to the barn. Just like he expected, one horse was missing.

He hurried to saddle Elvis up and was on his way.

The ride seemed to take forever, much longer than he remembered. The wind was stronger today though, which meant he knew he was headed in the right direction before he even caught sight of Clara or Edgar.

"Motherfu———" The wind shifted, stealing the sound of Clara's voice, making it cut in and out. "Son of a———"

"——king piece of sh——"

Edgar saw him first, the traitor immediately nudging his person to alert her they were no longer alone.

Clara spun toward him, her wide eyes immediately narrowing.

He'd loved her as the sweet and soft woman caring for his daughters like they were her own.

Appreciated her as the patient disciplinarian to the more defiant of his daughters.

Adored her as the mother willing to sacrifice anything to give her son a better life.

But the woman glaring at him was no one he'd seen before.

Her hair was wild, lifting around her head at odd angles as the wind carried it just like it had her colorful words.

Her cheeks were flushed. Her shoulders were straight.

Her chin was tipped high.

She was fucking magnificent.

Brody dismounted, dropping to the ground a few yards in front of her. "Seems like something's bothering you, Darlin'."

Her head tilted in the same way it did at the restaurant earlier. "Ya think?"

At first this seemed like a brilliant idea. They could work through whatever had her upset and go back home together.

Stronger. More connected.

Now he was realizing he might die instead. End up buried in the very place he led her to.

"I'm sorry." It was the easiest thing to do in these kinds of situations. Just apologize for it.

Whatever *it* was.

One dark brow lifted. "What are you sorry for, Cowboy?"

Yeah. He was a dead man.

"I'm sorry I upset you." It was difficult as hell not to ask it like a question.

He'd been with a strong woman before. Married her even.

Kept her happy.

He hadn't expected Clara to be like Ashley, but he also hadn't expected her to be so different.

Not more or less, just different.

And that meant he was in completely uncharted territory.

"What did you do that upset me?" She slowly began walking his way, her hips swaying in a way he'd struggle not to notice at any other time.

Who in the hell was he kidding? He was struggling not to notice them now. They might be the last thing he saw as a breathing man.

"Would you like me to help you?" Clara stopped a few feet in front of him. "I had things under control."

"It wasn't about things being under control. It was about a man disrespecting you."

"It was about him saying exactly what I knew everyone would." Her nostrils flared. "And you made it worse."

"I'm not the kind of man to stand by and let another man threaten my—"

"Your what?" She came closer. "You should probably think that through before you answer."

"Don't need to." Brody took the rest of the space between them in one step. "I've already thought it through long and hard, Darlin'." He wrapped one arm around her waist, pulling her body against his. "You're mine."

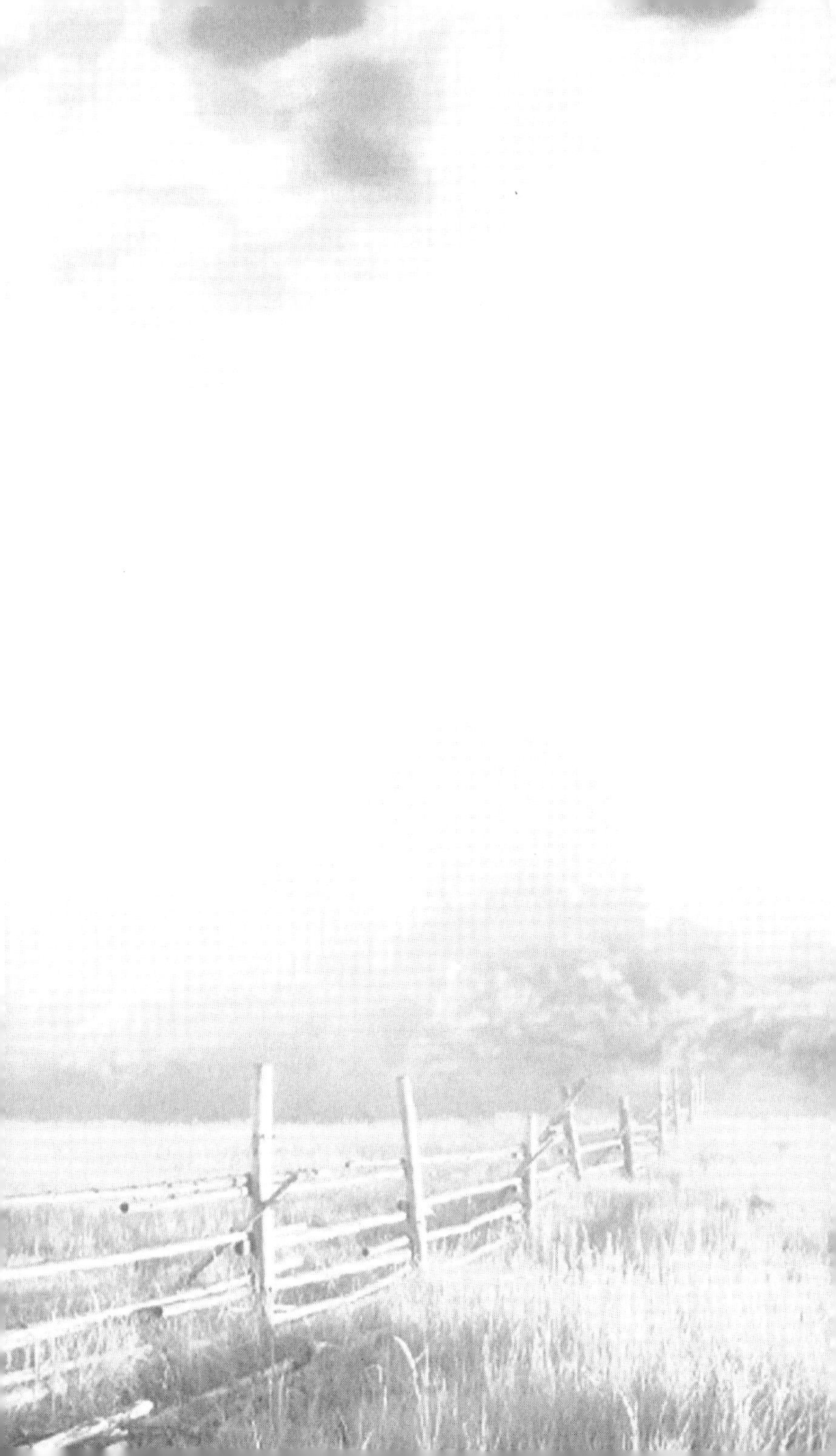

CHAPTER FIFTEEN

"AND HOW DO you see that playing out?" How could Brody not see the way this was going to end?

She would be the woman who slept her way into a job and he would remain untouched.

Maybe even end up admired.

Because that's the way it always went. Men could do whatever they wanted, leave women, and abandon children. Screw anything they wanted.

No one blinked an eye.

Not a woman, though. "Everyone assumes I'm having sex with you."

He had the balls to smile. "You are."

"They think I slept with you to get the job." Clara shoved at him and Brody let her go.

"Who cares?" He followed behind her as she walked away.

"I care." Clara turned to face him, stalking toward the man ruining her chance at a new life. "This was supposed to be our new home. Wyatt was supposed to finally be happy."

"Wyatt *is* happy. This *is* your new home." Brody stood still, letting her come at him. "This is where you belong."

"Great." She scoffed. "And now everyone here thinks I'm a whore."

"You think because one asshole ranch hand tried to figure out a way into your pants that means everyone believes the bullshit he fed you?" Brody closed in on her. "He is a piece of shit that just wanted to get a reaction after you shut him down."

Clara held Brody's gaze as he leaned down, lining his eyes up with hers.

"I'm happy to tell you how this is going to go if you want to hear it, Darlin'." He tipped his hat back, freeing space for his face to ease closer to hers. "But I'm not sure you're ready for how I plan on making sure this plays out."

"I can tell you exactly how this will go—"

"I don't think you can." His lips curved in a slow smile. "But I'm happy to listen if you want to get it off your chest."

"Don't act like you're humoring me."

"I am."

"Why in the hell did you come out here if you're just going to piss me off more?" She'd come out here to get away from him. To take some time to figure out how she felt before facing him down.

Or not.

"I came out here because this isn't how we're going to do things, Darlin'." He lifted his brows. "If something happens that upsets one of us we figure it out together."

"We're not a team, Brody."

His smile lifted a little more. "You sure about that?"

"Yes." It sounded like she was positive in her answer.

Which was good. Because she was.

"Seems like maybe you don't know how a team works then." Brody reached up to run one finger under the line of her chin. "You help me take care of my girls."

"That's my job."

"Fair enough." His finger slid along her skin. "I help you take care of Wyatt."

Clara scrunched her lips together, pissed that there was no way to argue that point.

"I've got your back no matter what." His eyes skimmed over her face. "And I'm willing to bet you've got mine."

She didn't have anything to say to him. She'd been angry at Dick a million times over the years. Never once did he hunt her down and insist on talking about it.

It was always swept under the rug and never discussed. She was just supposed to get over it and somehow she always did, stuffing it away.

"I don't want to talk about this." Clara tried to dart around Brody, but he snagged her arm before she could get anywhere.

"Nope. No one's leaving until we figure this out."

"There's nothing to figure out."

"Like hell there's not." Brody used his hold on her arm to turn her his way. "I can be patient. I can wait until you're ready, but I'm not pretending I don't fully intend on heading where I'm heading." His hand was firm on her arm but gentle. "And we're staying here until we figure this out together."

This was so much more than she bargained for. More than she was prepared to handle.

Clara yanked her arm free, turning toward the rolling

hills. "Damn it!" The sound of her words coming back wasn't as satisfying as it had been a few minutes ago. She spun back Brody's way. "You make me fucking crazy, you know that?"

"Now we're gettin' somewhere." Brody tipped his head. "What else?"

She shoved a finger in his direction. "You just go around doing whatever you want because you know no one will say shit about you because you're fucking Brody Pace." She tossed her hands up as she said his name. "You don't even think about what it'll be like for me." Her arms dropped. "For Wyatt."

That took the wind out of her sails.

It's what all this boiled down to. She couldn't care less what Duke the Dick thought of her.

But his opinion was probably shared by at least a few other people, and it was only a matter of time before it edged into her son's life. Tainted the fresh new world Wyatt already loved.

"Is that really what you believe? That I don't think about how what we're doing will affect you and Wyatt?" His head slowly turned to one side. "Because if you do, then you should sure as shit tell me to ride my happy ass back home and to never so much as look your way again."

"I didn't say I didn't want you to look at me." She pressed one hand to the uncomfortable squeeze in her chest. "I just don't want Wyatt to be the one who suffers because of my selfishness."

"You think wanting to be happy makes you selfish?" Brody snorted out an unamused chuckle. "You think that's what Wyatt wants? For you to be alone?"

"It's not about what Wyatt wants. It's about what he

deserves." She should have remembered that from the beginning. Then she wouldn't be here, trying to press away the knot tightening around her lungs as she tried to figure out how to stop what she'd started.

"What Wyatt deserves is a father who wants him." Brody's gaze was sharp as it met hers. "A father who puts him first."

"I can't change Dick." She'd tried. Worked for years to act just right. To be as invisible as possible, hoping at the very least Richard would notice their son and at least look his way.

"This isn't about that piece of shit." Brody pointed to her before turning the finger back on himself. "This is about you and me, Clara." His tone softened. "I can't make Dick be there for Wyatt, but I can sure as hell show up for him."

The tightness in her chest moved up, lodging in her throat.

"Just like you show up for my girls."

It was something she thought of every time those blonde-haired girls looked her way.

They would never know their mother. She would never know them. It colored every interaction she had with them. Made her want to give them what they deserved to have.

And offer what she hoped their mother would have wanted. Be what Ashley never had the chance to be.

"You pay me to show up for them."

"Don't you dare try to pretend what you do for my girls has anything to do with a paycheck, Clara."

She pressed her lips tight together. This wasn't about how she treated his daughters. This was about—

Hell.

What was it about?

"You want to give my girls the same thing I want to give Wyatt." Brody's voice was a little quieter as he came to stand right in front of her. "The question is, do you want to give me the same thing I want to give you?"

"What do you want to give me?" The words slipped out on a whisper that was almost lost in the breeze.

Brody smiled, his mouth lifting in the way she'd struggled with from the very first. "I want to give you the life you deserve."

She came out here to be mad at him. To revel in her anger before stuffing it down so she could ignore it the same way she had for the past ten years.

And he ruined it.

"I don't know what I deserve." It was a truth even she wasn't expecting.

Her focus had always been on Wyatt. What was best for him. What he deserved.

Her own happiness wasn't even a consideration.

"I do." Brody sounded more certain of those two words than she had been of anything ever.

Her life wasn't built on certainty. Its foundation was crafted on actions done out of survival, not with purpose or intent.

"If you want me to give you the same thing back, then you're going to be very disappointed because if I don't know what I deserve then I sure as hell don't know what you deserve."

Brody's smile held. "You're more than I deserve, Darlin'." He eased a little closer, his hands slowly coming to her face. "But I plan on doing whatever it takes to have you anyway."

"I NOT TIRED." Leah's eyes were red-rimmed as they stared up at her, tears edging the corners.

At least so far the girls were taking turns having tantrums. Breaking her into the twin dynamic a little at a time.

"Then you can just relax, but it's bedtime." Clara had already read the evening's story and tucked Wyatt and Michaela into their respective beds. Leah was the only hold out.

"I got her." Brody hustled through the door, his usual jeans replaced with the shorts he always wore to bed. "Come here, Little Monster." He scooped Leah up out of the bed in the room where Clara was staying and headed for the hall. He turned on his way out, shooting her a wink.

She sat on the edge of the mattress, staring across the room as the soft lull of Brody's voice filtered in, the words familiar.

He was reading to her.

The same book she read Wyatt every night until the twins became a part of their routine.

Clara closed her eyes, listening to Brody read to his daughter, knowing they were tucked into his bed, snuggled close.

He was the kind of father everyone should have. One who worked hard, but knew his job didn't end when the workday was done.

He showed up for his girls.

And now he wanted to show up for Wyatt.

That wasn't entirely true.

Brody already did show up for her son. Every day.

"Damn it." Clara shoved up from the bed, going to grab her pajamas from the chest before tiptoeing down the hall to the bathroom she shared with Wyatt. One hot shower later she was still in the same spot.

Stuck.

She flopped back onto the bed, pulling out her computer and firing it up, hoping to distract herself from the current situation she was in.

After browsing the internet for a minute she opened her email.

Ads and unwanted spam filled her inbox. Filtering through them made her feel a little better. Like she was at least straightening out one area of her life.

Until she came to one that wasn't an ad or spam.

But was most likely just as unwanted.

She opened the message from Cliff, scanning the few lines of text from her attorney before clicking on the attached document.

"Clara?" Brody stood in her doorway, his gaze filled with concern. "What's wrong?"

She'd been looking for a distraction.

And here it was.

"Dick's attorney sent a letter saying he won't press the paternity case if I agree to his terms in the divorce." She fell back against the headboard, tipping her head up to stare at the ceiling. "I knew this was what he was going for, I just didn't realize he had the balls to come right out and say it."

"Can he come right out and ask for that?" Brody closed the door and came in, going straight for the computer.

She turned it to face him. "Seems like."

He scoffed as his eyes scanned the screen. "I can't believe his attorney would do this."

She shrugged. "I guess he's getting paid and as long as it's not illegal he doesn't care."

"It's unethical though." Brody closed the laptop and shoved it across the bed, his body immediately taking its place as he sat in front of her. "He can't do this."

"Maybe not the way he's trying to, but at the end of the day he can force the paternity test." She blinked the tears trying to fight free. "He's such an asshole."

"You could be done with him."

She dropped her eyes to where Brody sat. "I wish."

"I'm about to suggest something I don't think you're going to like, but hear me out." Brody scooted closer, resting his hands on her knees. "What if you use the paternity test as leverage?"

"For what?" The only thing she wanted from Dick was for him to finally be held responsible for what he'd created, and the only way to do that was to make him pay.

Literally.

"Tell him you won't pursue a paternity test if he agrees to sign away all rights to Wyatt."

She sat up straight. "What?"

Had he lost his damn mind? All of this was about forcing Richard to take responsibility for the son he didn't deserve.

To try to get Wyatt something from the man who disappointed him at every turn.

"He's never going to be what you want him to be, Clara. He's never going to give Wyatt what he should."

"But he should have to give him *something*. I can't just let him walk away and pretend like Wyatt doesn't exist."

"Why not? Will it help Wyatt any if Dick has to pay child support? He's not going to do anything more than that. Hell, he'll probably keep fighting it just to be a pain in your ass."

"But Wyatt—"

"Wyatt is okay. He has a mother who loves him more than anything. He is taken care of and protected and wanted." Brody leaned closer, his eyes holding hers. "He will be just fine if you let Dick walk away." Brody reached out to slide his fingers down her cheek. "Maybe even better."

She knew what abandonment felt like. Knew how it shaped a child.

An adult.

"I'm not sure that's true."

Brody shifted, stretching out onto the mattress beside her like he was settling in for something. "Why do you think that?"

The question held no judgment, just curiosity.

She didn't share her life with anyone. People didn't understand.

Which made sense.

But he'd given her so much of himself. Of the past that shaped him.

"My mother was an addict." Clara's gaze dropped to her lap. No doubt Brody would look at her differently after this. Everyone did.

Somehow what she came from seemed to taint her in other people's eyes.

Made them either pity her or be certain she'd find the same fate due to the link of genetics.

"She would disappear for days at a time when I was little."

"Who took care of you?" Brody reached across her, wrapping his arm around her waist and pulling her closer.

"My grandmother." She dared a peek his way. "Until she died." Clara looked back toward the ceiling. "Then I was on my own."

"When did your grandmother die?"

This was the part she struggled with. The part that dictated all the decisions she made.

"When I was Wyatt's age."

CHAPTER SIXTEEN

THE THOUGHT MADE his stomach turn.

A little dark-haired girl with Wyatt's eyes all by herself, not knowing when the person who was supposed to love her most would return.

It was almost impossible not to react to this revelation, but that was what Clara needed from him now.

She didn't need his anger. Or his frustration.

She needed his understanding.

"She walked away from me over and over." Clara fingered a spot on her knit pajama pants, rubbing over it as her eyes went far away. "She didn't want the responsibility." She swallowed, the sound of the action proving the difficulty of it. "She didn't want *me*."

This wasn't just about making Dick pay.

"Not everyone is cut out to be a parent, Clara."

"Then they shouldn't have children." The conviction in her voice hinted at the woman he knew she was deep inside.

The woman who continued on, even as the world

crashed down around her, threatening to bring her down with it.

She kept going anyway. Kept fighting through.

For her son.

Because to her, that's all that should matter.

"Being a parent is a choice." Brody reached for the hand still digging at the fabric covering her thigh. He slid his into it, lacing their fingers together. "Unfortunately some people decide against it too late."

Her eyes finally came his way. "So what then? Children are just supposed to suffer for their parents' indecision?"

That's why she wanted to force Dick to take responsibility. Clara didn't want Wyatt to suffer the way she had.

"They don't have to suffer, Clara." Brody scooted closer, needing to soothe the pain still aching inside her. "Not always."

She sucked in a breath, blinking up at the ceiling. "I'm not sure there's another option."

"There is. I promise there is." He reached up to brush the hair off her face. The skin of her cheek was hot. Damp. "And I can prove it if you let me."

Clara's lips rolled in, pressing tight together.

"Look at me."

Her head barely shook.

"Please."

Her eyes slowly lowered to find his.

He wasn't prepared for what was there to greet him.

Pain. Pure, unhindered pain.

Regret.

Sadness.

All the things she locked away. Kept hidden somewhere she thought they would stay.

"It's never too late, Clara."

It's why she fought him so hard. Why she tried so desperately to keep him away.

Not just for Wyatt.

And not just because of him.

Brody held her eyes, refusing to look away from the gift she gave him. Honesty.

The truth he'd been seeking.

"Come here." He reached for her. She came easily, her soft body rolling into his, her head coming to rest against his chest as he pulled her close.

He pressed a kiss to her hair, letting his lips linger, breathing in the soft scent of the shampoo he'd used to wash it the night before.

He did it to show her he could take care of her.

Would take care of her.

Always.

But he hadn't realized exactly how much Clara might need that. How little care she might have been shown.

It made his chest ache.

His throat tight.

This woman who cared so much, who loved so deeply, had never felt it given back.

And so she fought it.

Because it was the only safe thing to do.

The only way to protect a heart that had been broken too many times.

He kissed her again, this time resting his lips on the

clammy skin of her forehead, keeping them there as he breathed her in.

Tried to calm the upset inside him.

Right now hers was the only upset that deserved his attention.

Clara's head tipped, dark eyes coming to find his.

They held. Looking.

Searching for something he hoped she would find.

An answer he hadn't yet learned how to give her.

Slowly they lowered, falling from his.

But not far.

Her gaze moved over his face, down to his mouth, catching on the scar Boone gave him before his younger brother left nearly a decade ago. Clara reached up to stroke across the nearly invisible spot on his lower lip.

She leaned in, brushing her lips against it with a whisper of a touch. Brody held perfectly still as she lifted from his arms, even though all he wanted was to pull her back.

Tuck her close. Prove he could protect her from all the things that haunted her. Past and present.

But this woman didn't want his protection. She didn't want him in front of her fighting the demons that lingered.

Clara pressed her palms to his chest, eyes skimming lower as she came over him, thighs pressed at each side of his hips, knees sinking into the mattress. Her fingers trailed down his sternum, over the fabric of his shirt. Slowly they began to gather it up, bunching the soft cotton together until his stomach was bare.

She pushed the shirt up, over his chest, until it stalled out, caught under his arms.

Brody lifted, reaching back to grip a handful between his

shoulder blades, pulling it up and off before lowering back to the pillows.

Clara's eyes followed the path of her touch as it moved over his skin, soft but steady. She traced the jagged white line across his ribs, dug there by a barb of wire on a fence he didn't quite clear at fifteen. Her fingertips moved across the deeper cut on his stomach, this one surgical in nature. The result of an emergency appendectomy when he was ten.

She found the tiny scarred bumps left from a case of chickenpox he and his brothers shared as kids.

"I knew you couldn't be perfect." Clara said it like it proved something important.

"I'm nowhere near perfect, Darlin'. I can promise you that."

She seemed to ignore him, lost in the focus of her eyes on his body.

When her fingers tucked into the waistband of his shorts Brody almost stopped her.

Clara's gaze came to his then. Like she knew.

It held as she worked down everything covering his lower half at once. Freeing the part of him that refused to hide his response to her touch.

She rocked back on her heels, taking him in with a slow drag of her dark eyes down his naked body. The weight of it was almost like a touch. Heavy and hot. Forcing him to close his eyes against it in an attempt to maintain control.

Sanity.

When her hands traced up his thighs he nearly jumped, every cell in his body rushing to focus on where her skin met his.

It was no longer so easy to close his eyes as her touch slid higher, the graceful line of her fingers a sight he couldn't resist as they curved against him.

Then around him.

He couldn't bite back the groan she took him in hand, those same soft fingers wrapping tight where he strained for her.

Clara's lower lip went between her teeth as she watched the glide of her hand over him, her already dark eyes turning nearly black as she fisted him in long strokes. Each one dragging his hips to her when she pulled away, an involuntary reaction to the loss of her touch.

"Clara." He was trying. For her.

But not touching her was torture. Not having the feel of her smooth skin under his hands.

His tongue.

Not hearing her cry out for him.

Brody reached for her, ready to do whatever it took to convince her to come to him. Let him show her what she tried so hard not to hear him say.

She was his.

He knew it the same way he knew the sun would rise again.

Clara was meant to be his.

But she didn't come to him.

Instead she undid him. Lowering her lips, the wet heat of her mouth sinking onto him, stealing the air from his lungs.

Thought from his mind.

It was gone. Thieved away by this woman who had no clue he was hers.

Bought and paid for.

Brody's hands went to her hair, lacing through the soft strands as she pulled him deep.

Watching her was hell.

Not watching her was worse.

She was glorious. Eyes shining with the power he'd longed to give her as they locked with his.

He would let her have it as long as he could. Offer up what she'd had so little of.

And she thrived on it, each move more sure, each stroke more certain.

Her full lips hugged him tight. The soft cheeks he stroked so often hollowed with every drag, each one pushing him closer to the place he would not go.

Not like this.

When he couldn't handle it anymore, Brody reached for her. "Stop."

"No." The response was sharp and strong.

A tit for tat.

One he probably deserved.

He'd own that.

Brody pushed up, reaching for her again, this time succeeding. He hefted her up, groaning as her soft body fell against his, before rolling, taking her to her back. "Yes."

He caught her fight with his lips, stopping any argument she most certainly had with the cover of his mouth, swallowing it down as he worked his hand into her pants, reminding her of some of what he had to offer.

That's what mattered most. Showing Clara what he so easily knew.

His fingers brushed against her heated skin, pressing deeper, finding her slick and wet.

Brody groaned against her lips as he stroked over her, the easy glide making his dick strain, making his skin feel too tight to contain the pressure there.

Clara pushed at her pants, shoving them down as she kicked her legs, working them free of the constraining barrier.

His own pants were still tangled around one ankle. Brody reached for the shorts, digging through the mess for the item stashed in the pocket. Once it was in hand he went for her shirt, wanting as little between them as possible.

Clara arched her back, pulling the shirt away on her own, her hair waved and wild as it fell free. Her skin was so smooth. So soft where it pressed his, making him loose a little of the hold he still had.

Brody made quick work of the condom, letting his wrapped cock fall against her, working his hips as he teased them both, stroking against her slit with his length.

Clara moved against him, doing her best to adjust the location of his thrust. "Please, Brody."

"You don't have to say please to me, Darlin'." He ran his nose along hers. "*Now*, Brody works just as well."

Clara's eyes locked his. "Now, Brody."

He reached for her, cradling her face. "So damn beautiful."

Her hand came to rest against his, pressing him to her as she leaned into his touch. "Now, Brody."

He couldn't stop the low chuckle. "I thought you'd be more patient than this."

"You thought wrong." Clara reached between their bodies, gripping him tight as she lined them together.

And lifted her hips.

He gritted his teeth against the desire to thrust deep, remind her how well he filled her.

"Now, Brody." It was half demand, half plea.

And it snapped the tiny bit of restraint she had not yet severed.

He pushed into her, hard and fast. The dig of her fingers into his skin and the pitch of her soft cry pushing him farther from the control he so desperately needed.

But he'd never had much control when it came to her.

Clara made him want everything.

And she made him want it now.

This moment was no different.

Brody reached between them, knowing his time was limited, finding her clit with the pad of his thumb as his mouth found the straining peak of a breast. He worked them like his life depended on it.

It seemed like it did.

Her nipple was tight under his tongue as he pulled it deep, working in time with the piston of his hips. Everything narrowed until all he knew was the feel of her under him. Around him.

In his mouth. Under his hand.

His lips broke from her breast, face pressing tight to her skin as he fought the need to come. The need to hear her come because of what he gave her trumped any want he had.

Clara's thighs tightened against his hips. Her nails bit his skin. Her soft cries gained volume. He lifted his mouth to hers, smothering them out, making them his as she bowed under him.

One.

Two.

It was all he could manage before he was gone.

Lost to her. Like always.

Holding her close. Like if he just held tight enough she wouldn't try to go again.

Wouldn't try to keep running.

Not that he wouldn't keep chasing her if she did.

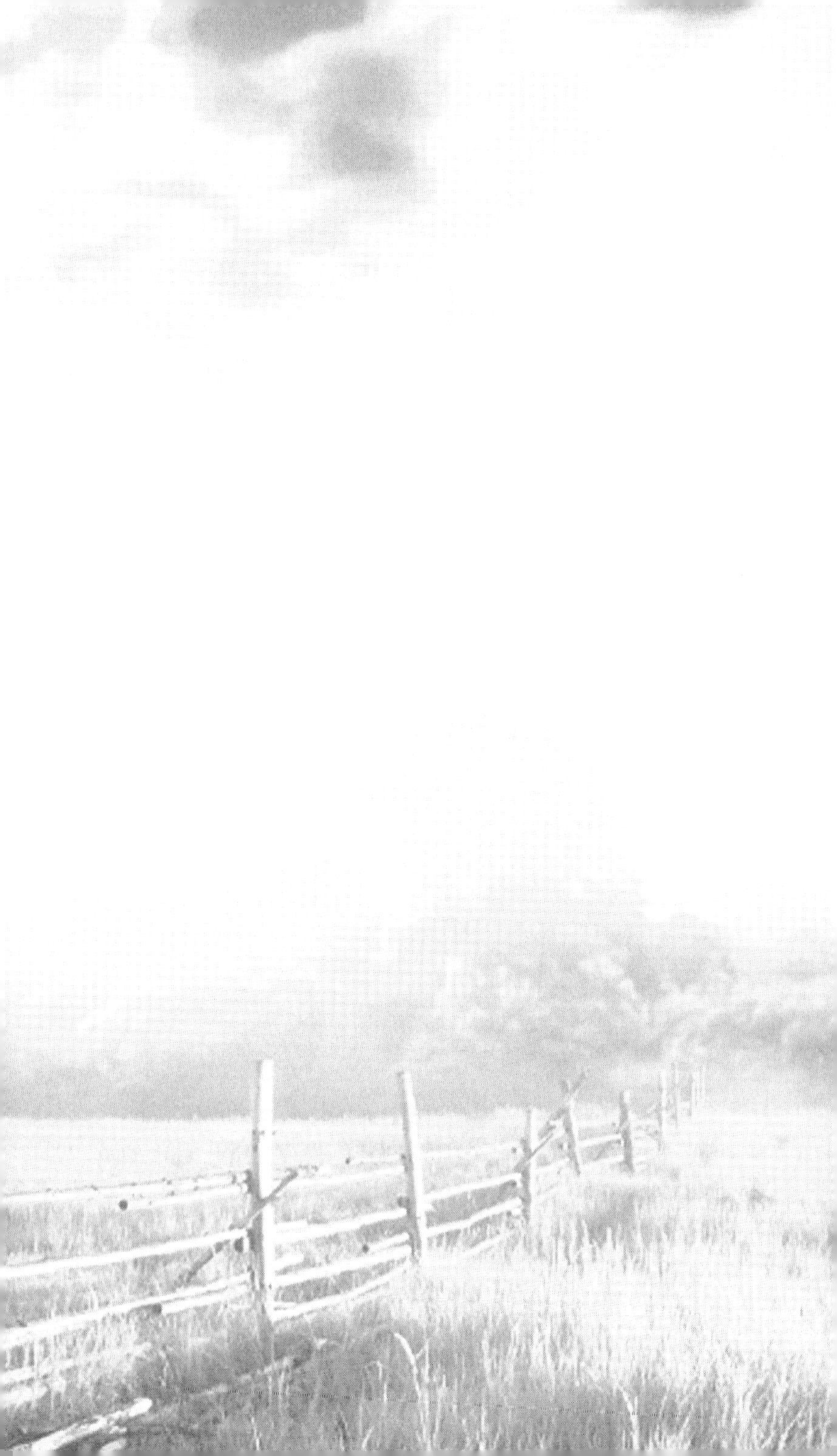

CHAPTER SEVENTEEN

"WHAT DO YOU think, Little Man?" Brody led Wyatt along the line of horses in the stable.

Clara watched as Wyatt reached up to brush his fingers along the nose of a dapple-gray mare. "Whose horses are these?"

"They're all mine." Brody led them through the stable that housed the horses the family didn't use on a regular basis. "These are the horses the ranch hands use, but you need a horse of your own." Brody leaned against the stall where Wyatt was stopped. "It's time for you to have your own horse to ride."

The mare dipped her head to sniff at Wyatt knocking the brim of his hat to one side as she checked him out.

"This here is Abigail. She's been on the ranch her whole life." Brody pulled an apple treat from his pocket and passed it off to Wyatt.

Wyatt held the snack out for the horse, smiling as she carefully took it from his palm.

"I think she likes you."

Wyatt ran his hand along Abigail's cheek. "She's pretty."

"You want to try her out?"

Wyatt's eyes went wide. "Right now?"

"Gotta do it sometime." Brody flipped the latch on the gate to Abigail's stall, pulling it open and leading the smallish horse outside. A few of the ranch hands were milling around the stable and the adjacent cabins. She'd been past the cabins before, but this was the first time she'd seen them up close.

They were nicer than most of the places she'd lived in her life.

The door of one cabin opened and Brody's next-youngest brother, Boone, came out onto the small porch, his attention immediately coming their way. "You finding Little Man a horse?"

"Yup." Brody adjusted the saddle he strapped to Abigail's back. "I think he made a wise choice."

"Miss Abigail's one of the sweetest horses we've got." Boone came their way, patting Abigail's rump before holding out a fist for Wyatt.

Her son immediately bumped his against Boone's, each of their hands immediately exploding, sound effects and all. It was a move that Wyatt had clearly done before.

"Pretty soon you'll be out with us." Boone deftly worked his way down the stirrup on his side of the horse, checking everything in the same methodical way Brody did. "We can put you to work."

"Could I really help?" Wyatt watched Brody and Boone as they made sure everything was set.

"Round here everyone has to help." Brody stepped back. "Otherwise Miss Maryann won't keep feeding us."

"She makes good pie." Wyatt immediately stepped in beside Abigail.

"That she does." Brody explained the basics of mounting a horse to Wyatt, pointing out the proper places to hold and showing him the correct way to position your foot in the stirrup. "Got it?"

"Yup." There was no hesitation in her son. None.

"Have at it then." Brody stayed close, his relaxed demeanor making it seem like he had full faith Wyatt could handle it on his own.

But the focus of his eyes stayed right on her son. The man barely blinked as Wyatt talked himself through the steps Brody laid out for him.

Clara held her breath as Wyatt hefted himself up, managing to land in the vicinity of the saddle. Unfortunately, he overshot, and started sliding off the other side.

"Good job." Boone had him before Clara could even think about rushing in. The second oldest of the Pace boys smiled wide as he righted Wyatt's body, positioning him in the saddle. "You know it took your momma five tries to get on a horse?"

Clara scoffed.

"Really?" Wyatt pressed his hat into place, firming up its position on his head.

"Almost kicked Brody here in the—"

"Nope." Brody picked up the reins, passing them to Wyatt. "Remember what I said about how to hold them?"

Wyatt nodded, eyes still wide.

"Let's go then." Brody started walking, leading Abigail the same way he'd done with Edgar.

Abigail immediately followed, her slow walk even and measured.

"That's a good kid you got there." Boone watched with a smile that hinted at pride as Brody led Wyatt and Abigail around the yard in front of the cabins.

"Thank you." Clara smiled as Wyatt started moving along with Abigail, his small body rocking in time with the horse's steps.

"Heard you had a run-in at The Wooden Spoon."

It was the last thing she wanted to be reminded of right now.

Anytime really.

"It wasn't a big deal."

Boone relaxed back against the fence circling the pasture connected to the barn. "Sounds like it was a big deal." He kicked one foot back, hooking the heel of his boot over the bottom fence rung. "I talked to Ben Chamberlain from Cross Creek and he was real upset about what happened."

"It wasn't his fault."

"Doesn't matter. It was one of his men acting out. Means he feels responsible for what happened." Boone tipped his head. "That's how it works round here. We don't put up with bullshit and we own it when it happens."

"It's fine."

Boone studied her for a second before pushing off the fence. "Fine or not, Liza Cross will most likely come over to let you know she's sorry for what happened."

None of this was worth discussing anymore. It was actually something she'd prefer to forget. "Who's Liza Cross?"

"She's the owner of Cross Creek Ranch."

The attention she'd been trying to keep from the conversation snapped sharp. "A woman owns the ranch?"

Boone tucked a toothpick in between his teeth. "Women can do anything they want, Darlin'." He grinned around the bit of wood in his mouth. "They can run a ranch." He gave her a wink. "Or kick a worthless ranch hand's ass." He started to step away, pausing close at her side. "Unless someone steps in and steals her fun." Boone was still grinning as he walked toward the row of cabins, leaving her staring after him.

Who in the hell had he talked to? Mae maybe?

"Mom! Look." Clara turned to find Wyatt grinning from ear to ear as he rode Abigail her way.

"Where's Brody?"

"He said he'd be right back but that I should bring Abigail back here." The horse stopped in the exact spot where she started, her ears flicking as she waited to see what would be asked of her next.

Clara reached out to stroke across Abigail's cheek. "She's a pretty horse, isn't she?"

"I think I like her." Wyatt smoothed down the long hair of her mane. "Do you think she likes me?"

Abigail seemed calm and easygoing. She probably liked just about everyone.

But Wyatt didn't need to know that.

"She does seem to be really happy right now." Clara reached into the pocket of her shorts and pulled out one of the snacks she always kept on hand, holding it out for the horse who was about to be her son's new best friend. "You have to be sure to listen to everything Brody tells you, okay?"

"He's real smart with horses." Wyatt went quiet for a minute. "Mom?"

"Hmm?" She glanced up when Wyatt didn't immediately answer. "You okay?"

"Yeah." He gave her a little shrug. "I just really like it here."

"Good." Clara gave him a little smile.

"Are we going to be able to stay?"

"Of course we can stay." Clara stepped closer. "This is our new home."

"We had to leave our home before."

"That was different." Her chest tightened as she struggled to explain what made it different. "I work here. This is not just our home. This is my job."

"What if they kick us out?"

The sadness in her son's voice cut into the ache between her ribs, slicing deep into a wound she'd carried as long as she could remember. "If they decide they don't want us here then we will be just fine. I promise."

Coming to Red Cedar Ranch had seemed like the answer to her prayers. A single solution for the list of problems she had.

It never occurred to her that a single answer would also mean one single change would rip it all away.

Her income.

Their home.

Their security.

The family Wyatt was beginning to feel attached to.

All of it could be gone at once.

———

"SEEMS LIKE YOU'RE not the only natural rider in the family." Brody stepped into the room, his hair still damp from the shower he snuck away from story time to take.

"That's good." Clara was already in her bed, the covers tucked tight around her, computer perched on her lap.

She did her best to keep her eyes on the screen instead of the man standing shirtless in the doorway.

"Clara." Her name was slow and easy as it came out of his mouth. "Something's bothering you."

He didn't ask. Normally he asked.

"I'm just tired." It was easier to not tell him the truth. Easier to not consider the truth herself.

Brody shook his head slowly from side to side. "No." His mouth pressed into a considering line before he let out a sigh. "I thought maybe we got past this."

It was almost impossible not to engage in the conversation, but the more she talked, the longer he would stay, and right now everything felt so—

"I know you think it's easier not to talk to me, but I can promise you it's not." Brody came into the room, his steps slow as he dragged one palm across the other, his eyes staying on her. "That's the only way this will work. If we talk to each other."

"So there's only one way this will work? That doesn't sound promising." Clara focused on the screen in front of her displaying any rental property within ten miles.

There weren't many.

Brody snagged her computer, turning it his way. He scanned the open window, his brows lifting as he let out a low whistle.

Clara grabbed the laptop back, pressing it closed before holding it tight to her chest.

He was going to be mad. Angry she was exploring her options.

And maybe that was best. It would stop this whole thing before it spun out of control and she and Wyatt were right back where they started.

Nowhere to go.

No one to trust.

But Brody didn't look upset at all.

His lips curved, lifting into a slow smile. "I thought I still had a few weeks before you decided to try to run from this." He leaned close, resting his hands on the bed beside her. "Figured you'd take a little more time pretending you didn't like me as much as you do."

Clara swallowed hard as his body pressed closer.

"Breathe, Darlin'." Brody's words were soft against her ear.

"I am breathing." She was not. She was stuck in some sort of version of fight or flight.

Or stay and fall in love with a cowboy.

"If you need space from me then I'll be the one to leave, Clara. Not you." Brody slowly dropped, coming to his knees next to her bed. One wide palm rested on her thigh. "I'll go stay with Boone until you're ready for me to come back." He lifted his brows. "But you and Wyatt aren't going anywhere. This is your home."

She shook her head. "No. This is your home."

"I can see how you'd feel that way." His thumb ran over the blanket covering her legs, the movement soft and soothing. "But I'm not sure my home is anywhere you won't be."

She squeezed her eyes closed, trying to shut him out in the only way she could.

"I'll go pack a bag."

The weight of his hand left her thigh, snapping her eyes open.

But Brody wasn't gone. He was still right there, still holding that same smile from earlier.

"But I'll be back in the morning to remind you why this is where you belong, Darlin'." He slowly stood. "Eventually you'll figure it out." He shot her a wink as he backed toward the door. "Goodnight."

Brody pulled her door closed as he left her alone.

Clara pressed the spot between her ribs, trying to ease the odd tightness there.

It was just from stress. The worry she'd been harboring, waiting for this perfect opportunity to implode.

But there had been no implosion.

She scooted her computer off her lap onto the bed and stood, a sudden tingly energy making her need to move around. It was familiar. It was what had propelled her through the past year.

What carried her through countless sleepless nights and long hours working so she could keep a roof over her head and food in Wyatt's belly.

But there was no waitressing job to occupy this restlessness. No papers to write. No checkbook to balance within an inch of its life.

She paced around the room, expecting the feeling to ease.

But it only got worse.

The room was hot. The air in it not enough to fill her lungs.

She went to the window and tried to lift the pane. It didn't budge.

"Damn it." Clara flipped the lock open and tried again, this time managing to get it up. The night air was warm as it filtered in. She dropped down and leaned her forehead against the screen, closing her eyes as she tried to slow her breathing.

Panic attacks were something she was familiar with. They'd been an unwanted friend for most of her life, but this was the first she'd had since coming to Montana.

The sound of whistling lifted her lids.

Brody strode across the gravel toward his truck, a bag slung over one shoulder. The tune he whistled was light and airy, continuing as he tossed his bag into the truck bed.

Suddenly he turned toward the house.

He was still smiling, and it widened the second his eyes landed on her.

Sitting in front of the window, watching him go.

"Damn it." She'd said that word more times in the past week than she had since Wyatt was born. "Stop smiling!"

"Not happening, Darlin'." He tipped his head her way. "I'll see you in the morning. Go get your ass in bed."

"Don't tell me what to do." Clara dragged down the window sash and dropped the blind into place. She'd never argued with a man as much as she'd argued with this one.

She'd never argued with a man period.

For the entirety of her marriage to Richard, what he said went. He had all the money.

That meant he had all the power.

And he loved to use it against her. Still.

It wasn't actually any different than her current situation. Technically Brody had the power to make or break her position. All he had to do was say the word and she would be out on her ass.

With nothing. Again.

But she wasn't the one leaving the house tonight.

And unfortunately, that was the problem.

CHAPTER EIGHTEEN

"I'VE NEVER SEEN a man so happy to be banished to the cabins." Boone sat at the tiny table in his cabin, pulling on his boots.

Brody stood in front of the bathroom mirror, shaving down the stubble he'd ignored last night in his haste to get to Clara, thinking he might finally manage to keep her in his bed until morning.

What happened was even better. "Didn't get banished. Came here on my own."

"I don't believe you." Boone stood up, stomping his feet to get the hem of his jeans into place. "No way would a man voluntarily leave a house with a woman like Clara in it. You did something to fuck up."

"You're wrong." Brody grabbed a towel and wiped down his skin, clearing away the bits of shaving cream clinging to his ears and lips. "Sometimes you gotta give a woman breathing room so she can think."

"Not sure that's the right approach." Boone came to stand in the doorway to the small bathroom at the back of the cabin. "She might realize you're not what she wants after all."

"I am what she wants. She just thinks it will all go to shit." Brody pulled his shirt over his head. "I need to let her figure out it won't."

Boone lifted a brow, scanning the black shirt as Brody tugged it into place. "Can you breathe in that thing?"

Brody grinned at him. "Worry about yourself."

He'd pulled out the tightest shirt he owned and packed it in his bag last night. Giving Clara space was important. She needed to see the truth he knew and she had to do it on her own.

But that didn't mean he wasn't planning to do everything in his power to hurry the process along. "Ready for breakfast?"

Boone shook his head, chuckling. "I'm ready to finally not be the only one on our mother's shit list."

"I'm not on her shit list." Brody grabbed his hat, settling it on his head as he walked to the door.

"I can guarantee you are." Boone dropped his own hat into place, following Brody out to his truck. "And I'm here for it."

"I didn't do anything wrong." Brody climbed into the driver's seat, starting the engine as his brother pulled the passenger's door closed.

"I'm not sure she's going to see it the same way." Boone rolled down his window, slinging one arm across the door as they headed to the main house. "And you know damn well she's going to take Clara's side."

"There aren't any sides." Brody shifted in his seat. "We're both on the same side."

Boone might be right. Maryann Pace was notorious for laying into her boys anytime they acted out of line, especially when a woman was involved. She tolerated no bullshit where that was concerned.

"You should see the look on your face." Boone pointed at Brody. "You know I'm right."

"I'll talk to her. Explain the situation." He could just tell his mom that Clara was having a hard time realizing that she was safe. That they had her ba—

Brody pulled the truck into its spot and turned to Boone. "Don't say anything to mom."

"Afraid my stink'll rub off on you?" Boone had been in the doghouse for almost a decade. Ever since he left to travel the country and live his dream.

"Nope." Brody climbed out of his truck, standing tall as he caught sight of his mother on the porch, arms crossed as she stared him down.

Boone was right. Maryann Pace did not see things the same way he did, and right now Brody was grateful as hell for it.

He just had to survive the next few days.

"Mornin'." Brody went up the steps, not missing the fact that his brother was hanging back quite a bit.

Who was worried about whose stink, now?

His mother's eyes narrowed. "Get your plate and take it out to eat in the barn."

"Yes, ma'am." Brody breezed right past his mother and into the house, heading straight for the kitchen. Clara stood at the fridge, Leah at her feet. Her eyes went wide as they caught his over the sippy cup she was filling with milk.

He shot her a wink.

A towel snapped him right in the ass. "Get your breakfast." Maryann stood between him and Clara, hands on her hips as she stared him down.

Boone came in and tipped his head Clara's way. "Morning."

"Morning." Clara passed the filled sippy cup to Leah, her eyes moving between Brody and his daughter. "Here you go."

"Fanks." Leah took the cup and wandered his way. "Daddy, can I has a bacon?"

"Sure thing." He passed a strip down to his daughter.

She took it and immediately went back to Clara, reaching her arms up. Clara hefted her onto one hip and Leah's head immediately dropped to Clara's shoulder, bacon in one hand, cup dangling from the other.

Clara watched him with a wary gaze as he finished filling his plate. The second it was full his mother pointed to the door.

Brody immediately went the way she indicated, going out into the back and toward the barn. He dropped to the grass, stretching his legs out in front of him as he leaned back against the red cedar siding. He was almost through his plate of food when he caught Clara's eyes through the window.

He gave her a smile.

It was easy to do. This morning couldn't be going better if he'd given his mother a script.

Luckily Maryann Pace was about as consistent as it got. He and his brothers had a habit of making her life difficult when they were younger, and it led her to always assume they were in the wrong.

To be fair, she was usually right.

Not this time though. This time Brody was doing exactly what he should be doing.

Showing Clara the truth of what her new life was really like.

"HOW LONG YOU gonna ride this out?" Boone tossed back the covers on his single bed.

"As long as it takes." Brody fell into the other twin-sized bed in the small cabin.

"You better hope she's not as stubborn as she seems then." Boone stretched out, his feet reaching the very edge of the mattress. "Cause these beds suck."

"It'll be worth it." Brody shifted around, trying to get comfortable. "You could always get your own place, you know."

"You know damn well I can't do that." Boone slung one arm over his eyes. "That would just piss Mom off more. She'd never get over it then."

"It's been six months since you got back. She might not get over it as it is." When Boone came home it was clear his younger brother thought things would go back to the way they were. That he'd be able to move right into his old room and resume life on the ranch as he knew it.

Maryann Pace wasn't having it.

Not that she had to outright say it. Brooks and Brett were already in the nice cabin, built as the boys graduated and wanted their own space. The idea for a Nanny came right as Boone moved back, and the other two bedrooms in the house were quickly earmarked for whoever that nanny would be.

Which conveniently left Boone to the row of cabins for the ranch hands.

"At least I have a cabin to myself." Boone tipped his head to look Brody's way under the drape of his arm. "I *did* have the cabin to myself."

"Sorry to cramp your exciting life as a bachelor." Brody eyed the tiny bed Boone laid in. "Can't imagine any women being too excited to share that bed with you, though."

"Haven't tried." Boone's eyes were back under the cover of his arm.

"That explains your bad attitude." Brody leaned up to switch off the lights in the cabin. "Maybe you should start tryin'." He dropped back to the bed sitting less than six feet from his brother's. "Just don't do it until I'm back in the house."

"You're awful confident for a man who's been out here almost a week."

Brody pulled the covers up to his chin. "I sure am."

He'd just started to fall asleep when a light knock sent him sitting straight up in the bed.

"I got it. It's probably one of the hands needing toilet paper." Boone hefted his body up.

"It's not." Brody shoved his brother out of the way as he went to the door. Just before pulling it open he chucked his shirt, tossing it to one side.

No reason not to stack the deck in his favor.

He slowly opened the door, the sight of Clara on the small porch making his whole body relax with a relief he didn't know was waiting for him.

"Hey there." Brody leaned one arm against the frame of the door. "Everything okay?"

"You know damn well it's not okay." She glared at him in the dim light of the moon, arms crossed tight to her chest. "You're doing this on purpose."

"Absolutely I am." Brody grinned out at her. "I tried telling you the truth but you wouldn't listen. Had to show you."

"I should tell your mother."

Brody straightened, stepping out onto the porch and pulling the door closed at his back. "You haven't already?"

"Of course I haven't told her. She'd kill you." Clara took a little step back as he eased closer.

She was protecting him. Clara might not want to admit it, but she definitely had his back. "So what's your plan now, Darlin'?"

Clara went silent.

"So you came all the way here just to argue with me?" He moved closer, following as Clara continued to back away from him.

She scoffed. "No."

"Seems like you did." Brody leaned in as her behind bumped into the railing surrounding the porch, resting his hands at each side of her body. "So let's argue."

"I don't like to argue."

"You didn't used to like to argue." He took a breath, the air moving easily in and out. Because everything was easier when she was there. "I think I'm getting you comfortable with the idea."

"People shouldn't argue."

He laughed. "Who in the hell told you that?"

Her lips pressed tight together in a move that immediately dampened his blossoming good mood.

"I'm gonna tell you something right now, Darlin', and you can take it however you want." He dipped his head so his eyes were level with hers. "You can bet your ass anything Dick said is complete bullshit."

Every time he thought he'd reached the peak of wanting to kick Dick Rowe's ass, something managed to make it worse.

"People argue all the time. It's not the argument that makes the difference. It's how you do it." He reached out to run his fingers across her cheek. "We're different people, Clara. We're going to think different things. I always want to know what you think. Even if it's different from what I think." He smiled. "But I'm not saying I won't try to persuade you to see things my way."

"Is that what this was about? Persuading me to agree with you?"

"No." Brody caught a little of her hair, sliding his fingers along the dark strands. "This was about you seeing the truth." He worked his way a little closer. "I wanted you to see this is your home no matter what you choose when it comes to me."

"But if I don't choose you then your mother will make you live out here."

Her concern for him smoothed down the sharp edges ready to cut Dick Rowe deep enough to make him bleed forever. "I don't live in the main house because that's my only option, Darlin'. I can easily build my own house."

"Is that what you would do?" Her eyes slowly dropped from his face, easing down his bare chest.

"That's what I'll be doing either way."

Her dark gaze jumped to his. "Either way?"

"I don't plan on staying in the main house if you decide you'd be happier without me." Brody shook his head a little. "And I sure as hell don't plan to stay there if you decide different."

Clara blinked up at him, the full line of her mouth dropping open a little.

"Don't look so surprised." He smiled. "I'm a grown man, Darlin'. I'm old enough to know what I want and I'm smart enough to recognize it when I see it." Brody was more than ready to lay it all out for her, giving Clara the full truth he'd held back until now. "And I'm not going to apologize for being ready for what I want."

He could almost hear her swallow. "What are you ready for?"

"All of it. Rings and weddings and anything else I can get you to give me."

"I just wanted you to come back to the house."

Brody tapped her on the chin. "And that there's why you're in charge." Brody leaned in a little closer. "Cause if it was up to me we'd be making all sorts of plans already."

"I'm still married."

It was a tiny hiccup. A minuscule inconvenience in their immediate future. "Not for long."

Her lips rolled inward, sliding together as her eyes once again dropped his.

He could feel the shift of Clara's mood immediately. Like someone flipped a switch, sending her from the woman he knew to the woman Dick smothered and controlled into a shadow of herself. "What did he do?"

Her eyes lifted, resting on the underside of the roof hanging over the porch. "He sent another letter requesting the paternity test. This one went through the courts." She sniffed a little, her chin lifting higher. "It has a date I'm required to comply by or I can be held in contempt."

He was trying his damnedest not to push her too hard. Trying to let Clara see what he knew on her own.

But damn it was hard to hold back when shit like this kept happening.

Brody immediately wrapped his arms around her, pulling Clara close. He tucked his head close to hers, breathing deep.

He couldn't tell her it would be fine.

It wasn't.

He couldn't tell her not to worry. That wasn't a fair request.

And he sure as hell couldn't fix this for her.

All he could do was be there. Right behind her to remind her she wasn't the woman Dick tried to make her into.

"We will get through it, Darlin'."

Her arms came around his neck as she sniffed once more, her face pressed into the crook of his neck. "Please come back to the house."

CHAPTER NINETEEN

"WHAT IN THE hell are you doing here?" Maryann glared at Brody as he stood in the doorway to the kitchen.

"I went and dragged his ass back here last night." Clara took a sip of her coffee as she leaned back against the counter.

Maryann's brows lifted as she turned toward Clara. She blinked once.

Twice.

She might have thrown his mother for a loop with that one.

"You wanted him back here?"

Clara smiled at him over the rim of her cup. "For now."

Now it was Brody's brows that raised.

She might just keep everyone on their toes from now on.

It was more fun than she anticipated.

"I'd like to take a trip into town today. Maybe get Wyatt some school clothes." She held his gaze. "Would you care to join us? I think the girls are ready for some new pants for the fall."

"I would enjoy joining you in anything you do, Darlin'." He slowly came toward her, his lips twitching with the threat of a smile.

Clara held out the cup of coffee she'd poured him after sneaking out of Brody's bed. "We'll see about that."

Maryann finally turned from where she'd been watching them, going back to the gravy she had cooking in the giant skillet on the stove.

Brody took his coffee with a wink. "Thank you."

It caught her a little by surprise. "You're welcome."

She'd been with Dick for almost ten years and he'd never once thanked her for anything, including the child she carried and cared for.

"I'm going to go get the girls up and moving." He backed toward the stove, stopping to press a kiss to his mother's cheek as he passed.

"Mmm-hmm." Maryann watched him go before turning back to her gravy.

Clara took a deep breath and stepped in at Maryann's side. "I thought if things didn't go the right way you would fire me."

She'd been up half the night trying to figure out what to say to the woman who hired her. The woman she cared for as more than a boss.

There was only one conclusion she could come to. Maryann deserved an explanation.

Maryann's head snapped her way. "Why in the hell would you think that?"

"Why would you want me here if I made your son uncomfortable?" It was still a question Clara struggled to understand the answer to.

"Because my son is grown and knew the risks when he decided to step out of line." Her expression was serious. "Brody knows how things work around here. He knew damn well where it would land him and decided you were worth the risk." Maryann's lips twisted into a sly grin. "Not that I'm upset at the choice he made."

The last bit made Clara pause.

"Don't look so shocked, Dear. I knew there was a chance at least one of my son's would try to snap you up." Maryann went back to stirring her gravy. "And I can't pretend like I'm not tickled to death at the thought of things working out." She turned back Clara's way. "But you listen to me. No matter what happens I intend to keep you and Wyatt here at Red Cedar Ranch. It's where you belong."

It was the same thing Brody told her more than a few times. It was something Clara felt, deep down in her soul.

But it never felt real. Like this place could really be her home.

Like it could really be hers.

Not until now.

Clara wrapped both arms around Maryann, squeezing her tight. "I'm so glad I came here."

Maryann managed to get the arms Clara accidentally pinned to her sides loose enough to hug her back. "Oh, honey." She patted Clara's back. "I am too."

"What's wrong, Cla-la?" Michaela padded across the floor toward them, hustling straight toward Clara, arms lifting as soon as she was within grabbing distance.

"Nothing's wrong." Clara scooped the little girl up, tucking her close. "Did you see Nana is making gravy for breakfast?"

"I like gravy." Michaela leaned toward Maryann, the blue eyes that matched her daddy's so closely fixing on the skillet. "I can has some now?"

"Almost." Maryann turned Clara's way, resting one hand on Michaela's cheek before pressing the other to Clara's. "Such sweet girls."

Michaela turned to look at Clara, giving her a grin so wide it squinted her eyes. "Love you Cla-la."

The simple statement lodged right in Clara's throat. Michaela wasn't old enough to really understand what she was saying, but still.

After all the tantrums and difficulties they'd gone through in such a short amount of time, Clara expected the little girl would probably come to like her less. It was a hard pill to swallow, but worth it if it helped Michaela move through this difficult age and come out a happier, more secure little girl on the other side.

That's what tantrums were about. Insecurity. Fear. Disruption.

And the thought of Michaela feeling any of those things broke her heart. "I love you back."

"I know dat." Michaela kicked her legs, ready to be back on the ground to run wild. "I'm going get Leah." The second her bare feet hit the wood floor she was off and running.

"Can you get the girls set up at the table?" Maryann glanced at the clock on the wall. "The boys'll start coming in any minute."

And just like that they were right back to normal. No weirdness. No awkward silence or conversation.

Just business as usual.

"On it." Clara grabbed the twins' favorite sippy cups and

went to work filling them with milk. By the time she was done both girls were racing into the kitchen, Michaela with a stuffed bear dangling from one hand and Leah dragging her daddy along.

"Come get your milk and go sit in your seats." Clara passed off the cups and turned, ready to get the twins' plates filled and in front of them.

A warm, wide hand came to rest on her back. "I got it, Darlin'."

She stiffened a little as Bill came in, his eyes immediately coming to catch where Brody's hand rested. The older man didn't miss a beat, immediately tipping his head Clara's way. "Morning."

"Good morning."

Bill scanned the kitchen. "Where's my boy?"

"Wyatt's in brushing his teeth. He'll be down in just a minute." Brody moved from her side, walking along with his dad to where Maryann was setting up the line of food for the morning meal. "I told him he could come out with us tomorrow."

"He's been working real hard on his riding." Bill grabbed a plate. "I think he's ready to start learning the ropes."

It was something she never expected to come from this. The possibility that the people who hired her would not just take her in as one of their own, but also her son, was never anything that would have occurred to her.

But that was exactly what they'd done.

———

"WHAT DO YOU think?" Wyatt did a slow spin in the open door to the dressing rooms.

"Move around. Make sure you got enough room to be comfortable." Brody dropped to a crouch and rocked side to side. "They shouldn't feel tight."

Wyatt immediately did just as Brody was, his eyes sticking to Brody like glue as he repeated the move. "I think they're okay."

"Go get changed back then." Clara glanced down at the pile of clothes Brody had stacked up, doing a mental calculation as she eyed the stack of clothes. For the first time in years she had money of her own to spend as she wanted, but her savings was nonexistent, and spending so much at once simply was not something she wanted to do.

There were still attorney and court costs stacking up, and it appeared she would continue to be the sole provider for her son for the foreseeable future. That meant she had to be careful. Wyatt needed new clothes, that wasn't up for debate, but the purchasing of them would have to be spread out. Clara pulled out a few pairs of jeans and a handful of the shirts, draping them over her arm. "I think these are my favorites."

"Good to know." Brody took the stack from her, piling it back on top of the rest. "How's it goin', Little Man?"

"I'm puttin' my boots on."

"Cla-la, I'm firsty." Leah sat in the front seat of the double stroller the twins probably wouldn't fit into much longer.

Clara pulled Leah's cup from the diaper bag that held snacks and drinks and items to entertain the girls instead of actual diapers. "Do you need to potty?"

Leah looked down at her lap. "I fink so."

"Let's go then." Clara lifted the tray boxing the little girl in.

"I has to potty tooooo." Michaela lifted her arms high over her head.

Two girls in a public bathroom did not sound like any sort of fun, but neither did having to strip one down after she peed her pants. "Okay." Clara pulled Michaela free.

"Wyatt, Buddy. Put a wiggle in it. We gotta take the girls to the bathroom." Brody dropped the pile of clothes onto the now-empty stroller.

"It's fine. I'm sure we can handle it." Clara held one little hand in each of hers. "Right, girls?"

"I'm sure you can handle it too." Brody gripped the handles of the giant stroller. "But we're a team, remember?"

She'd taken Wyatt to the bathroom literally every time he'd ever been when he was little. If by some chance Dick was with them, he never offered a word of assistance, let alone followed along to help.

Wyatt rushed through the door to the dressing room, the jeans he just tried on dangling from one hand.

"Toss 'em on top." Brody pushed the stroller along, Wyatt sticking by his side as they made their way to the back of the store where the bathrooms were situated. He parked the stroller right next to the door of the ladies room and picked Michaela up, turning her toward the pile of clothes. "Which pants are your favorite?"

Clara took full opportunity of the distraction, pulling Leah into the bathroom while Michaela temporarily forgot she also wanted to potty. Luckily the stalls were clean and decently-sized, making it easy to position the toddler in the way least likely to result in wet pants.

Regular-sized toilets were not made for small bottoms.

She had Leah redressed and her hands washed in record time, ushering her out to where Brody stood. They traded girls and Clara repeated the process.

Michaela swung her legs as she looked around the stall. "This is better than the daddy one. It smells bad."

Had he been doing this alone for three years?

She got Michaela's shorts back up and washed both their hands before going back out to where Brody was passing one of the fruit bars she packed to Leah. "I think they're a fan of shopping with you." He grabbed Michaela and settled her back into her seat before handing her a fruit bar of her own. "I don't pack snacks."

"They're hush money." She'd always taken Wyatt everywhere she went. Richard didn't have any interest in watching his son, so that meant if she wanted to go somewhere, Wyatt went along too.

Doctor's appointments. Grocery shopping.

Meetings with her attorney.

But she'd been so caught up in her own realities she sort of forgot to think about Brody's.

Maybe she wasn't the only one who'd never been part of a team. He did have his family to help him, but that wasn't the same thing.

He might have had his mother to watch the girls while he worked, but other than that it seemed like Brody handled everything else on his own.

"What would we do without our Clara?" Brody reached

into the bag and pulled out the granola bar she'd packed for Wyatt. "You want something too, Little Man?"

Wyatt took it with an odd smile. "Thanks."

"Don't thank me. Your momma's the one who takes care of all of us."

She swallowed, the action more difficult than it was a minute ago.

No one had ever acknowledged what she did. "It's not a big deal."

"You think." Brody unlocked the brakes on the stroller. "I'd have two screaming little girls by now if it was up to me." He pushed the stroller toward the registers, Wyatt close at his side.

He only took two steps before turning around and holding one hand out to her. "Come on. Let's get checked out so we can go home."

Clara swallowed again, this one even more difficult than the last. She glanced to where Wyatt stood, making faces at the girls, laughing as they cackled.

She took Brody's hand and stepped in at his side.

He leaned over to press a kiss to her temple. "Just breathe, Darlin'."

Maryann was a difficult enough hump to get over.

But Brody's mother was only one of many. There was Wyatt. The twins.

His brothers.

The people in town who would think—

"Hey there." Mae from the restaurant stood at the checkout Brody lined up in. She smiled brightly at Clara, her eyes dipping to the stack of clothes. "You girls need to quit growing so fast."

"We're big." Leah held up her fruit bar. "Want some?"

Mae pressed one hand to her belly. "I actually just ate." Her eyes were warm as she focused on Leah. "I appreciate the offer though."

"Fancy meeting you all here."

Clara turned toward the deep voice at her back. Boone stood just behind her, a basket packed full of items hanging at his side. He tipped his head, the expression on his face changing almost instantly. "Mae."

Boone's expression wasn't the only one that turned different. Mae's formerly warm and open smile flattened in a heartbeat, turning into a full-fledged frown that perfectly matched the glare she shot Boone's way before turning to the cashier. As soon as her card was swiped and her receipt was printed, Mae grabbed her cart and turned to Clara. "It was nice to see you again. You should come visit me sometime." Her eyes moved to Brody and the girls. "You guys have fun. I'll see you soon." Then she spun away, never once acknowledging Boone's existence with more than that initial icy glare.

Clara was so distracted by the exchange she didn't notice Brody had piled everything onto the belt in one single spot until the cashier was halfway through the stack of clothes.

She reached toward them. "I—"

Brody caught her hand with his, tugging her close. "Wyatt needs these clothes so he can start helping us. I don't expect you to pay for him to learn how to help out."

Clara forced on a smile as Wyatt glanced her way. "I don't want you to feel like you have to take care of my child."

"You think I'm doing this because I feel like I have to?"

She didn't want to answer that.

Brody smiled. "That's what I thought." He turned, passing his credit card to the cashier before leaning close to Clara's ear. "I plan to take care of Wyatt for a long time, Darlin'." He straightened to take the card as the cashier passed it back. "If you decide to let me."

CHAPTER TWENTY

THERE MIGHT AS well have been smoke coming off her skull for how hard Clara was thinking.

She sat in the passenger's seat of his truck staring out the window as Wyatt and the girls sat together in the back sharing the bag of cheese crackers from the diaper bag.

"Boone and Mae were together all through high school."

As he hoped, the revelation was enough to bring her attention his way. "Mae dated Boone?"

"They more than dated." Brody relaxed a little, stretching his arm across to rest one hand on the back of Clara's seat. "Everyone thought they'd get married."

"Mae didn't seem too fond of him."

"Not now, no." Brody smiled. "She hates his guts now."

Clara snorted a little. "She doesn't try to hide it."

"Mae doesn't try to hide anything now."

"Now?" Clara's brows lifted. "What do you mean *now*?"

"Mae was real sweet in school. Real quiet." He glanced Clara's way. "Wasn't one to speak her mind or cause any sort of problems."

"She still seems sweet." Clara's voice carried a defensive edge.

"She is. She's one of the kindest women I know." He smiled a little. "But she doesn't put up with any bull from anyone."

"Good for her."

"It is good for her. If she'd married Boone she'd probably still be that same quiet girl who didn't stand up for herself."

Clara's eyes slid from his, drifting back to stare out the window.

She was back to thinking. At least now she had more to chew on.

Hopefully enough to help his cause.

His mother was on the porch when they pulled up, sitting in one of the rockers.

And she wasn't alone.

"Who's that?" Clara eyed the other woman through the truck's windshield.

"That would be Liza Cross." Brody opened his door and jumped out of the truck, circling round to open Clara's door as she continued to study Liza. "Why don't you go sit with them and chat while I get the kids out?"

"I can help." Clara unbuckled her belt.

"I know you can." He grabbed her around the waist and hauled her out of the truck.

Clara slapped at him. "What are you doing?" Her eyes went straight to where Liza and his mother were watching.

"Darlin', I'm tellin' you right now, most people aren't going to find you and me bein' together as interesting as you think they will." He pressed one hand to the small of her back, urging Clara toward the porch. "Go get some iced tea and sit with them. You might be surprised what you find out."

She shot him a downright hateful look over one shoulder, but Clara did as he all but made her do, walking toward the porch, her soft summery dress floating along with her.

Liza and his mother both stood as she approached, wide smiles on their faces.

He knew exactly what Liza came for, and it centered around the woman walking their way.

Brody went to work unloading the kids, pulling Leah from her seat and putting Wyatt in charge of her before unbelting Michaela and grabbing all the bags, passing each girl a lightweight one, and Wyatt one for each hand. They walked together toward the porch where, as he expected, Clara was already seated between the two other women, a glass of tea in her hand.

He tipped his head Liza's way. "Afternoon, Ms. Cross."

"Afternoon, Brody." Liza gave him a smile. She was less than five years older than him, but due to a shitty set of circumstances, she was the only surviving member of the Cross family.

A family she married into.

And that meant she was the one left in charge of Cross Creek Ranch.

Wyatt tipped his head toward Liza. "Afternoon, Ms. Cross."

Clara's eyes immediately came to Brody's before dropping to her son. She shoved the glass of tea to her lips, drinking it down as she blinked her eyes a few times.

"Aren't you just a gentleman." Liza's hand went to her

heart. "That's from having a momma who's raising you right." She pointed his way. "You're a lucky boy."

"Yes, ma'am." Wyatt gave Liza a smile. "Thank you."

Maryann Pace's head dipped in a slow nod as she rocked in her chair. "You girls have fun shopping with your dad and Clara?"

"Cla-la packed snacks." Leah held up the bag that still had two single crackers in it.

"That's because she takes good care of you girls." His mother continued her rocking. "Why don't you take your daddy in the house and get ready for lunch?"

He knew when he was being dismissed, and his mother was an expert at it.

But leaving Clara on her own didn't sit well. He knew this conversation would help Clara feel more at home here in Moss Creek.

But she didn't know that.

He caught Clara's gaze. "Do you want me to handle that situation for you?"

It was an out he hoped she understood. There wasn't much for him to work with in this scenario and it was the best he could come up with.

She gave him a little smile. "That would be fine."

"If you change your mind just let me know."

Clara's smiled widened. "Okay."

Brody tipped his head to Liza. "Nice to see you."

"You too." Liza was one of his favorite people in Moss Creek and one of the best for Clara to get to know. They had more in common than Clara realized, and Liza's story would definitely settle any lingering fears Clara had about how the town would look at her.

Michaela was already racing through the house, ready to burn off the pent-up energy from being good for such a long time. Brody set the bags on the table and snagged her as she ran by, rolling her up in his arms to blow a raspberry against her chubby belly. "You were awful good today at the store, Little Monster."

Michaela cackled, her chubby hands fighting her shirt back in place so he couldn't continue to tickle her.

"I was good too." Leah frowned up at him.

"Does that mean you want me to blow on your belly too?" He dropped Michaela to her feet and started chasing Leah around the house. Brody almost had her when he caught sight of Wyatt watching them around the corner.

"Hey." Brody pointed Wyatt's way. "Let's get Wyatt and tickle him."

Wyatt's face immediately split into a smile. "No." He took off running.

But not trying to get away.

Michaela reached him first, taking him down like only a little girl with three wild uncles could, grabbing him around the thighs and throwing all her weight against him.

Leah was on the pile immediately and both girls had their fingers dug into Wyatt's ribs and armpits.

"What in the world is going on in here?" Maryann stood in the entryway, an empty pitcher of tea in one hand as she stared at the pile of kids on her living room floor.

"Tickle fight." Brody took the pitcher. "I can fill this for you."

His mother snatched it back. "I've got it."

He glanced toward the porch.

"She's fine. Otherwise I wouldn't have left her." Maryann

headed toward the kitchen. "Come help me get lunch started."

"WANT ANOTHER ONE?" Brody held out the cracker and cheese stack.

Clara shook her head, letting it rock against the back of the glider. "I'm good."

"How about everything else? You good there too?" Clara had been more quiet than normal since her talk with Liza today and he wanted to be sure she was okay.

Clara looked out over the stretch of land across the back of the house. "Liza seems nice."

"She is nice."

"Can I ask you a question?" Her head rolled his way. "It's sort of personal."

"You can ask me anything you want, Darlin'."

She paused, pursing her lips a little. "Why didn't you and Liza get together?"

"She reminds me of a younger version of my mother." Liza was no-nonsense and straightforward. She took no shit from anyone ever and made no apologies for what she was.

But she would give anyone the shirt off her back if they needed it.

Probably because of all she'd been through.

"I like your mother."

"I do too. Doesn't mean I want to marry her." Brody tipped back a drink of water, grimacing as he swallowed it down. "I think I just grossed myself out."

Clara laughed. "Fair enough." She went quiet for a minute. "She asked me to lunch."

"You gonna go?"

Clara shrugged. "I think I have to."

He didn't like her thinking she still had to do things she didn't want to. "You don't have to do anything."

"I didn't mean it that way." Her brows came together. "I meant I have to for me." Clara's eyes came to him. "Does that make sense?"

"It does." Brody scooted down in the glider, resting his head next to hers and kicking his feet up on the edge of the little table in front of them, using it as leverage to keep them rocking. "She and Mae are best friends, so I'd expect Mae to be there too."

"Liza and Mae are best friends?" Clara smiled a little. "Huh."

"Huh?" He reached over to rest one hand on her thigh.

"I guess I just never thought about it." Clara's head dropped to rest against his.

"Never thought about them being friends or never thought about friends in general?" He had a pretty good guess which one was correct, and it was one more reason he knew Moss Creek was where Clara should stay.

"I guess I forget what it's like to have time for friends." She shifted around, resting more of her body against him.

"Now you can remember." Brody turned his head to press a kiss to her hair. "It's time for you to start living your life, Clara. To be happy."

She rested her hand on top of his. "It's strange to think about."

Brody closed his eyes, soaking in the moment. He

understood where she was coming from. For so long all he could do was tread water. Working and taking care of his girls was all there was.

But then they got a little older and he could breathe a little.

Enough to start thinking about the future. How he wanted it to look.

"It was strange for me to think about being with someone besides Ashley for a long time." There were many days where he never thought it could happen.

The thought of all she would miss out on was smothering, blanketing out anything but pain and regret.

And guilt. Guilt that he would be there for all of it. That he would get to see their daughters grow up.

"Tell me something about her." Clara's fingers traced across the back of his hand.

"You really want to know about my dead wife?"

"I want to know what I can tell your daughters about their mother." Her fingers continued their slow drag over his skin. "She deserves for them to know her."

Brody swallowed at the tightness in his throat, clearing it once before trying to answer. "She was a teacher. She read to the girls every night while she was pregnant. Was convinced it would make them learn to read faster."

Clara's head tipped as her eyes lifted to his. "But you didn't keep reading to them."

He shook his head. "I couldn't." Brody turned his hand, lacing his fingers with hers. "That's how I knew you were supposed to be here. When I saw you reading to them."

It's not that he thought some unearthly presence brought Clara to Red Cedar Ranch.

But it was plain as day that she was meant to be theirs.

"I knew from the beginning that no matter what happened, I wanted you and the girls to be together. If I had to move to the cabins to make that happen then I would have."

"I thought you were going to build a house to live in."

"Well—"

Clara sat up, twisting to face him. She jabbed at his ribs with one finger. "Don't act like you were willing to sleep on a twin bed forever."

He tried to catch her poking finger as she moved it around, stabbing different spots with a surprising speed. "I shouldn't have told you that."

"Too late now, Cowboy." Clara squealed as he finally caught her, pulling her across his lap.

Her smile was wide and relaxed as she stared up at him.

"I'm gonna tell you something, and it's only cause I know you're gonna need a minute to get used to the idea."

One brow lifted. "Brody Pace, you better not—"

"I have every intention of getting you to marry me, Darlin'. Come hell or high water I plan to do whatever it takes to make it happen."

Her head dropped back. "Why do you do this to me?"

"It's your fault. You should probably try to be more of a pain in the ass. Make me reconsider."

It wouldn't change anything. Hell, he'd probably only try to make it happen faster if she got feistier.

And chances were good if Clara started hanging out with Mae and Liza that's exactly what would happen.

"You'd like it." She came back at him, this time full-on ready to tickle him.

"Damn straight I'd like it." Brody grabbed her around the waist, hefting her up as he pushed off the glider, stumbling a little as it shifted under him.

Clara yelped, grabbing onto him as he slung her over one shoulder like a sack of grain. "If you drop me I'll—"

"You'll do what? Tell my mother?" He grabbed the screen door. "Better be quiet or she'll come out and see me carrying you up to my bed."

"You're the one who'll get in trouble." Clara whispered it as he walked through the kitchen toward the stairs.

"And yet you're still being quiet." He went up the stairs as fast as he could, keeping his steps quiet as he snuck past the kids' rooms. Once the door to his own room was kicked closed he rolled Clara off his shoulder and onto his mattress. "Because you don't want me to end up back in the cabins."

Her frown was as sexy as everything else about her was. "Stop gloating."

"Nope." He leaned over her. "I'm gonna gloat about catching you until the day I die, Darlin'."

CHAPTER TWENTY-ONE

"YOU'RE GOING TO have fun."

Clara stood in front of the closet in her room, flipping through the options.

There weren't many. She could probably use a shopping trip herself.

One without Brody. Otherwise he'd try to buy half the store.

Brody was stretched out across the queen-sized bed behind her like he owned it. Technically he did.

A fact that bothered her slightly less than it used to.

"I should have put them off until next week." Clara pulled out a long dress she hadn't worn since coming to Moss Creek. It wasn't practical for chasing little girls or riding horses, which were the two main things she'd been doing lately.

That and—

"What is that?" Brody pushed up off the mattress and stalked toward her. "Why have I not seen you in that before?"

Clara shoved the dress back into place. "Because I'd trip on it and kill myself trying to wrangle your daughters."

He grabbed the hanger and pulled the dress free again, his blue eyes skimming down the length of the fabric. "You need more dresses like this one."

Clara snatched it away from him. "Again, I will end up on my face trying to do my job."

It was something she tried to always keep in the front of her mind.

This was still her job.

And she was sleeping with her boss's son.

Her head dropped back as her eyes went to the ceiling. "I can't do this."

Brody's hands came to her shoulders, warm and solid as they rubbed down her arms. "You can do anything."

She straightened to look at him. "You're the first person to ever tell me that."

"Doesn't mean I'm wrong." Brody eased closer, his wide body barely resting against hers. "Look at everything you've accomplished. All completely on your own."

She huffed out a breath, shoving at him. "Fine. Get out so I can get changed."

"When are we going to tell the kids?" He held onto her, pulling her along with him as he moved toward the door. "I don't want to keep sneaking around them."

"I need to deal with one thing at a time." Clara rested her hands on his chest. "I need to get through this lunch and then figure out what in the hell I'm going to do about Dick, and *then* I can think about what to tell Wyatt."

"Maybe I should be the one to talk to Wyatt. Man to

man." Brody's lips quirked. "Maybe I should be the one to talk to Dick too."

A few weeks ago it might have been tempting to let someone else deal with Dick and his bullshittery.

"Definitely not. Dick is my problem. I'm the one who has to deal with him." It was an unfortunate fact. One she tried to ignore since it made her feel a little sick to her stomach.

"But Wyatt?" Why did Brody sound hopeful that she would let him be the one to explain the situation to Wyatt?

"Maybe." The thought of Wyatt having a man in his life like Brody was too much to consider at the current moment. "Now get out." She gave him another little shove and closed the door.

Clara pulled off the shirt and shorts she wore, folding them and setting the pile on the bed before sliding the dress over her head. The floral fabric was soft and flowy, giving it a sort of ethereal feel. It wasn't expensive or fancy, but it made her feel pretty every time she wore it.

Maybe Brody was right. Maybe she did need more dresses like it.

After strapping on a pair of sandals she yanked open her door, jumping back a little at the sight of Brody. "Why are you still here?"

His gaze darkened as it slid down her body. "I wanted to be the first one to see you."

It seemed like it took forever for his eyes to finally come back to hers. "You are beautiful."

His choice of words was almost as surprising as his presence had been.

Clara smoothed down the front of the dress. "I like it too."

"It's got nothing to do with the dress, Darlin'." He wrapped her in his arms again, pulling her close. "It's all you."

It would be easier to just blow the compliment off. Shut it out like she'd tried to do with everything else Brody and his world offered her.

But it no longer felt fair. "Thank you."

"Nothin' to thank me for. It's the truth." His hand came to her face, curving against her cheek as his lips brushed hers. "You better go or you'll be late."

He caught her hand, pulling her toward the stairs.

Clara dragged her feet. "Where are the kids?"

"Wyatt is out with my dad learning how to work the holding pens, and the twins and my mom just left to go check on the progress at the inn." Brody's hand stayed in hers as they walked out the front door and to where her car was parked next to his truck. She hadn't driven it in what felt like forever.

There didn't seem to be much reason to leave the ranch.

Brody pulled the driver's door open, holding it as she climbed behind the wheel. "It's got a full tank of gas."

She rolled her eyes up at him. "You didn't have to do that."

"How else am I going to convince you to marry me if I can't prove I'll take care of you?" He started to close the door, stopping midway. "Go have fun with your friends. We'll be here when you get back."

Her friends.

Was it possible that might be one more thing she would find in Moss Creek?

Clara managed a smile as Brody closed the door. She started the engine as he backed away.

The fan was turned up full blast and hot air poured from the vents. Probably because Brody thought it would help cool down her small sedan when he went to fill the tank.

Too bad her air conditioning didn't work.

She pressed the button to lower the windows and let the breeze in.

Just as the air blowing at her face started to cool.

Brody gave her a wink as he backed toward the house. "Bye, Darlin'."

"Damn it." Clara pressed the button, glaring at him as the window slid back into place.

He was making this impossible.

The inside of her car was like a refrigerator by the time she pulled up in front of The Wooden Spoon. She'd gone a year without air-conditioning and she couldn't bring herself to turn it down. It was one more uncomfortably comfortable thing Brody brought into her life.

Liza stood at the entrance to the restaurant, a smile on her face. She was absolutely beautiful with light brown hair and a lean frame. She'd been in jeans and a t-shirt when Clara met her, but now the owner of Cross Creek Ranch was decked out in a short summery dress and a pair of wedge sandals that took her already substantial height to another level.

She looked like a freaking model.

"Hey!" Liza came her way as Clara walked along the sidewalk. The other woman immediately pulled her in for a tight hug. "I love your dress."

Clara tried to fight the self-conscious need to push off the compliment. They'd been few and far between in her life, and it was difficult to wear them in a way that fit. "I like yours too."

"I never get the chance to dress up, so when I do I take it and run with it." Liza angled one leg out, moving her foot from side to side. "I got these on the clearance rack at Target. Five bucks."

"No way." Clara pulled at the side of her dress, swishing it around a little. "Ten bucks at Macy's." She tucked her hands into the openings hidden in the side seams. "And it has pockets."

Liza's head bobbed in an approving nod. "I'm going to need to go shopping with you."

"What in the hell are you two doing?" Mae stepped out of the restaurant, her eyes immediately going to Clara's dress. "Does that have pockets?"

Clara nodded.

"Why is it so hard to find dresses with pockets?" Mae shook her head. "If men wore dresses someone would find a way to put a pocket in every damn one of them."

"Probably." Liza bumped Clara with her hip. "But we can't do our normal man bashing. This one's got herself a decent version."

"Better than his son of a bitch brother, that's for sure." Mae's nostrils flared. "Come on. Before I lose my appetite."

Liza grabbed Clara's hand, holding it as they went into the building, following Mae to the corner booth she'd sat in with Brody and Wyatt and the girls.

Mae scooted into one side and Liza scooted into the other, taking Clara with her. "I'm so glad you came." Liza grabbed the glass of tea already sitting in front of her. "I needed this."

"Me too." Mae leaned across the table toward Liza. "Clara already knows this, but I haven't had a chance to tell you yet." Her eyes narrowed. "I ran into Boone the other day."

Liza's hazel eyes narrowed. "I hope you mean with your car."

"No." Mae seemed disappointed.

"Did he try to talk to you again?"

"Of course." Mae crossed her arms over the flour dusted shirt she wore. "He clearly doesn't realize I've got nothing to say to him."

"Maryann makes him sleep in the cabins." Clara blurted out the only contribution she had to the conversation, immediately regretting the odd comment.

Mae's lips pulled into a satisfied-looking smile. "Good. I hope he's miserable."

"I mean, he doesn't have you, so..." Liza sipped at her tea again before turning Clara's way. "What about you? I know you have Mr. Wonderful now, but I'm sure you've got a stinker somewhere in your past."

"I guess." Clara wrestled with how to explain the truth of her situation. "I'm still technically married to it." The admission felt good. It might go over like a lead balloon, but putting it out there seemed to take a little of the bite out of it.

"Isn't that the way it goes?" Liza shook her head. "They don't want you but won't let you go."

"He has to let her go one way or the other." Mae glanced up as one of the waitresses dropped three plates off at their table, setting one in front of each of them.

"I don't suggest the other way." Liza unrolled the napkin

surrounding her silverware. "It's not as satisfying as it sounds."

"And you still have to clean up the mess when it's over." Mae glanced up, her eyes going straight to Liza.

"I killed my husband." Liza turned to Clara. "Shot him after he stabbed me."

Clara was stunned. "Wow."

"Figured I'd put it out there. Rip the band aid right off." Liza dug through the pile of pasta in front of her. "This looks good, Mae."

Clara blinked her stinging eyes as the shock of Liza's past settled. "Does that help?"

Liza glanced her way, a strand of pasta dangling from her lips. "Help what?"

"Just putting it all out there. Does it make it easier?" She'd hidden the darkness in her life for as long as she could remember, keeping it from everyone around her. Teachers. Coworkers.

Even her own son.

Liza set her fork down. "If you own it it's yours." Her lips lifted at one side. "And ownership is power."

The truth of Liza's words settled something inside her.

Dick owned everything they had. The house and everything inside it. The cars. All of it was bought with his money.

But she paid just as much for it.

"My ex-husband is a piece of shit."

Not Wyatt's father. No more pushing that ownership off somewhere more comfortable.

Dick was hers. She owned him.

"He's trying to force me to give our son a paternity test

because he thinks I won't do it." The story poured out of her. Pretty soon she was taking bites between sentences and even laughing at the ridiculousness that was Dick.

"Are you going to do it?" Mae bit off a chunk of the toasted bread served alongside the pasta.

It was something she'd been sitting on for too long. A decision she gave more power than it deserved.

"No." Clara shook her head. "But I think I'm going to make him sweat about it a little longer."

Liza gave her a slow nod. "Own his ass."

Clara smiled. "I do own his ass, don't I?"

Mae frowned as she picked up a forkful of pasta. "He prolly wants to marry that poor girl he knocked up too."

"I should drag it out just to save her from him. Maybe she'll get smart faster than I did." Clara swallowed down a few gulps of the lightly-sweetened iced tea. "I can't believe I stayed married to him as long as I did."

"Nope." Liza held one hand up. "None of that. We don't have regrets. Only learning experiences."

"Well I wish I'd learned faster." Clara fell back against the back of the booth. "But then I guess I wouldn't be here."

"That's right." Mae's gaze was more serious than it had been. "And sometimes the way you come out the other side is worth all the pain of what you go through."

"And you got Wyatt." Liza tossed her napkin over the empty plate in front of her. "And that sweet little button nose is worth all of it." She scooted Clara's way. "I gotta hit the ladies'. All this damn tea she gives me."

Clara stood up, letting Liza shimmy past her.

"I'm gonna refill it while she's gone." Mae grinned as she grabbed the pitcher from the table. "Good thing it doesn't have alcohol in it. One of us would have to drive her home."

Clara sat back in her spot as Mae disappeared into the kitchen. She closed her eyes and took a deep breath.

It felt like she'd dropped an actual weight she didn't realize she was carrying.

"Don't you look happy with yourself."

What the fu—

Her eyes snapped open.

She almost couldn't believe what she saw.

"Dick?"

Richard's nostrils flared. "What did you just call me?"

Clara blinked, surely she wasn't seeing what she thought she was. "What are you doing here?"

"One of us has to be the adult in this situation, and since you're refusing to sign the papers it would appear that falls to me." He snorted. "Like it always has." He reached out and grabbed her arm, pulling her hard. "Come on. We're finishing this now."

"What in the hell are you talking about?" Clara tried to pull free of his grasp, but his fingers only dug in deeper.

"You've dragged this divorce out long enough and I'm done with it." Dick yanked her toward the door, shoving it hard as he continued to wrestle her. "I should have known you'd make my life difficult. It's what you've always done."

Clara planted her feet and twisted as hard as she could, managing to get her arm free. "I make *your* life difficult?"

Ownership is power.

"You know what, Dick?" Clara glared at the man she used to blame for the ruination of her life.

Except it wasn't true.

Her life wasn't ruined.

"You are an awful human." She shook her head. "Like, really, really terrible." Clara scoffed a little as all the clouds she'd been lost in parted, revealing a clarity she never knew could exist. "You didn't deserve me and you sure as hell don't deserve Wyatt."

"*I'm* an awful human?" Dick faced her, stretching to his full height in a way that used to intimidate her into compliance. "Everything that's happened is your fault. Not mine."

"You are right." She said each word clear and strong. "Everything that's happened *is* my fault."

She finished the college degree she abandoned when Dick showed up and promised her a world he never delivered.

She raised a son who was kind and smart and empathetic and respectful.

She lived the past year on her own grit and determination.

And it was all her fault.

"Here." Mae was suddenly at her side. She shoved a cast iron pan Clara's way. "You might need this."

CHAPTER TWENTY-TWO

"I'M GONNA MARRY her." He'd held back on making any sort of direct declarations to anyone besides Clara, but it was getting harder and harder to toe a line that didn't have any reason for existing.

"You better." His mother didn't look up from the magazine she was flipping through. "Otherwise I have to figure out how to fire you."

"You can't fire me." Brody dropped into one of the kitchen chairs. "I'm your son."

"That didn't stop me from firing Boone." Maryann lifted the magazine, turning it to face him. "You think these would look good in the rooms?"

"I don't know what in the hell will look good in the rooms." He scanned the pile of magazines sitting on the counter. "Didn't you hire an interior decorator?"

"I fired him. He wanted to put antlers everywhere." She flipped the magazine back her way, eyeing the page. "I'll wait until Clara gets home. She'll know."

"How long do you think they'll keep her?" Brody glanced at the clock on the wall. She'd been gone two hours already.

"As long as they want to and you won't complain about it. The girl deserves to have some time to herself." His mother flipped the magazine closed, tossing it on top of the rest.

"I wasn't complaining." He was happy Clara was out making friends and enjoying the freedom she deserved.

He would just also be happy when she came back home.

"How do you think Wyatt will feel about you wanting to marry his momma?" Maryann came to sit next to him at the table.

"I'm going to talk to him about it." Brody leaned back in his seat. "I've still got to convince her to let me marry her, so I figure I've got time to warm Wyatt up to the idea too."

"He'll probably be easier to sell on it than she will." Maryann shook her head. "She's been through a lot with that asshole ex-husband of hers."

"He wants her to have a paternity test done on Wyatt." Just talking about it raised the temperature of his blood. "He's trying to get out of paying child support."

"What a pig." His mother crossed her arms. "I'd like to have at him. Just two minutes is all I'd need."

"He'd probably run if he saw you coming for him." His mother was always put together and proper, but the woman had a look that made a man want to turn tail and haul ass in the opposite direction.

"He would if he knew what was good for him." She turned her head his way, studying him. "What do you think she should do?"

"What I think she should do doesn't matter." He had one

place in Clara's situation and that was right behind her, ready to have her back when she needed him and staying the hell out of her way when she didn't. "But I'm not gonna pretend I'd be upset about Wyatt needing someone to be his dad."

"Doesn't take papers to be a dad, son." His mother tipped her head in a nod. "Wyatt needs a man to be his dad no matter what happens with the asshole."

"I can't imagine not wanting to be that kid's dad." Wyatt was smart and sweet. "He's one hell of a little boy."

"That's because he has a good mother."

"She's an exceptional mother." It was one more thing that drew him to her.

Because Wyatt wasn't the only kid in this equation. He had two daughters that would benefit from having a mother in their life. The kind who would do what needed to be done even when it was hard.

One who would love them even when they were difficult.

One who would always put them first.

One who would keep the mother they lost close to their hearts.

"Once the inn's done I'm going to have the crew start a new project."

His mother's brows lifted. "Oh? And what project would that be?"

"I need a house." It had been in the plan since the girls were born. He hadn't actually intended to stay here as long as he had, but it was easier on everyone to be under the same roof.

"What kind of house?" His mother turned to grab her stack of magazines.

"Clara can have whatever she wants. Doesn't matter to me as long as she's happy." He'd live in a damn cardboard box if it was what Clara wanted.

"Huh." His mother gave him an appraising once-over.

"What?"

She shrugged. "I wasn't sure you'd really thought this all through."

"You thought I'd put her in the position I have without thinking it over?"

"I thought you were lonely enough you might be blind to how this would affect her." Maryann gave him a soft smile. "I know you wanted someone by your side. I was worried that was all you were seeing. How well Clara would fill that spot for you."

"If that was all I was worried about I'd have already tried to put a ring on her finger." Hell. He'd have probably proposed to her the second week if that was all he had to consider.

But her needs outweighed his.

His mother straightened, her brows coming together as she looked out the window across the table from them. "What in the world is your brother doing?"

Brett was hauling ass across the grass, headed for the back door.

Brody was on his feet before Brett made it inside, crossing the kitchen as his brother flew through the door. "Come on." He turned and took back off.

They'd been through enough as brothers he didn't need to ask why. Didn't matter.

Brody ran right behind Brett as his youngest brother made a beeline for Boone's running truck. Brooks and Boone were in the cab, windows rolled down. Boone leaned out the open pane. "Hurry your asses up."

Brett grabbed the side of the bed and hefted his body up and over, dropping to his ass as Brody did the same. The truck started moving before he was fully seated, gravel slinging as the tires fought for purchase.

"What's going on?" Brody held the open back window with one hand and the side of the bed with the other as Boone took the driveway at a speed they'd done more than a few times in their youth.

Brett's eyes met his. "We're goin' ass kicking."

It was why their mother always assumed they were the ones at fault in every situation. They may have had a habit of acting before thinking in their younger days.

"Why?" Not that he wasn't up for kicking an ass that deserved it, but he was a father now.

Hopefully a husband again soon.

They were all grown men.

They shouldn't just go around dishing out their own version of vigilante justice. At least not without being sure it was warranted.

Brooks was turned in his seat. "Just get ready. We'll be there in a minute."

The ride to town usually took fifteen minutes, most of it through Pace land.

This particular trip was done in half the time, the truck racing at speeds that would earn Boone much more than a ticket.

He barely slowed as they peeled into town, the truck bouncing across the paved roads as they flew down Main Street.

Brett raised up to peek over the cab, one hand pressing his hat in place as the other gripped the side of the center window. "Hell." He smacked Brody as the truck tires screeched, the sudden stop sending their bodies against the backside of the cab. "Get out before they kill him."

Boone was already out of the truck, leaving his door open as he ran toward The Wooden Spoon. "Come on, come on, come on!"

Brody dropped to the ground, a chill settling in his stomach as his brothers all took off like their lives depended on it.

There was only one thing he could think of that would bring them to The Wooden Spoon, ready to remind Moss Creek what the Pace boys were capable of.

Maybe two.

And he wasn't wrong on either count.

Clara stood in front of the restaurant, looking just a beautiful as she had when he saw her pull away from the ranch.

But the woman standing straight and strong, chin lifted and eyes narrowed was not the same woman he'd sent off for her first lunch in town.

The man in front of her was yelling something, his eyes bulging as he ranted.

And then one hand jutted out in the direction of her arm, reaching like he intended to grab her.

"Oh hell." Brody ran faster as Clara's arms lifted, pulling back toward her shoulder.

A cast-iron skillet gripped tight in her hands.

She'd kill him with that thing. "Grab her." He hollered Brett's direction as his brother closed in on the scene.

"Which one?"

Mae stepped closer to the man screaming at Clara, the tip of a butcher knife pointed at his chest.

Liza stood at Clara's other side, a marble rolling pin clutched in one hand.

He pointed to the least threatening of the three. "Liza."

Brett all but tackled the owner of Cross Creek Ranch, dragging her away.

Boone stalled out as Mae turned his way, the tip of her knife following suit. Both his brother's hands went up. "Now, Mae. I know you probably want to use that on me, but hear me out."

Mae lifted a brow. "Why would I want to use this on you, Boone?" She turned the blade, her eyes looking down it. "It wouldn't be worth having to sharpen it again."

Clara's eyes suddenly came Brody's way. Her brows went together as she glanced at the men circled around her. "Are you kidding me right now?" She pointed at Brody. "Get back in your truck and go home. I've got this." Her eyes narrowed as they went back to the man in front of her.

The Dick.

"Darlin', I will do just about anything you tell me to do, but I can't do that." He edged around, working his way toward her. "I know it sounds like fun, but you can't hit him with that."

"I feel like I can." She adjusted her grip on the pan. "Yeah. It seems like I can do it."

"I know you *can*, but I'm not sure you *should*."

"Who in the hell are you?" The Dick turned his sneer Brody's way.

"None of your business." Clara reached out to smack

Dick's cheek. "Pay attention to me. I'm the one you're dealing with, Dick."

Boone's brows lifted.

Brett glanced Brody's way as Liza shoved free of his hold, moving right back in at Clara's side.

Brooks grinned as he leaned back against the shiny, expensive sedan parked along the curb.

Brody took a step back, stretching one arm across Boone's chest, taking his brother with him as he gave the women a little space. He eyed Dick as he went. "You should probably do as the lady says."

Dick snorted. "She's not a fucking lady."

Brody slid his eyes Clara's way, lifting his brows in question.

"Nope." She bounced a little on the balls of her feet. "If anyone gets to hit him it's me."

"Damn." Brody sighed. He waved one hand Clara's way. "Get on with it then so we can get home, Darlin'."

Dick's eyes raked over him, nostrils flaring. "This is what you went to after me?"

Brody scoffed, his attention on Clara. "Now?"

She shook her head. "Nope. He's mine. I own him."

Dick's head slowly turned Clara's way. "You own me?" He snorted. "You don't own shit, Sweetheart."

Clara's head tipped to one side. "I do, actually." Her lips lifted in a smile that looked a little wilder than Brody remembered it. "I own it all. All of it's mine." Her crazy-ish smile widened. "You. The life I thought I had. The person I used to be. I own it all."

"You've never had anything, Sweetheart. Not when I found you and sure as hell not when I left you."

Clara's smile shifted, the wild edge it carried disappearing in an instant. "I have the only thing that matters. I have Wyatt."

Dick's brows went together. "Who?"

Clara's smile flatted in a heartbeat, and the wild was back, this time in the eyes twitching as they stared Dick down.

She started to swing the pan.

Mae caught it almost immediately. "We should probably think about this." Mae looked over Dick like he was a bug she was considering squishing. "If you hit him with that he'll probably bleed all over the sidewalk and then we'll have to clean it up."

"I've got a power washer." Liza stepped closer. "Probably two."

Clara stared at Dick a second longer. Finally the skillet dropped to her side.

Brody immediately stepped in behind her, gently sliding the cast iron concussion maker from her hand.

"I want you to give up your rights to my son."

Dick smirked. "Consider it done."

Clara crossed her arms over her chest. "Your attorney can do the paperwork and send it to Cliff. I'm not paying for anymore of your bullshit."

Dick lifted a brow. "Is that the mouth you kiss your son with?"

Clara turned toward Brody, her eyes immediately landing on the cast iron. He tucked it behind his back just as she reached for it, shaking his head.

She turned back to Dick. "Why are you still here?"

Dick gave her a slick smile. "Glad you finally came to your senses."

Clara looked him up and down, her lip curling just a little as she did. "Me too."

Dick turned to the car Brooks still leaned against.

Brooks didn't move. "I don't need her permission to kick your ass."

Dick stood for a minute like he might try to press what little luck he still possessed, but finally he rounded the car, climbing into the passenger's side before worming his way across and into the driver's seat.

Brooks straightened as Dick started the engine. The brothers lined up along the curb, shoulder to shoulder as the car eased onto the one-way street.

Brett stood right next to Brody. "It's less fun when we're not the ones running someone out of town."

"They're better at it, though." Boone turned to glance Mae's way. "We wouldn't have given two shits about the blood."

His brothers weren't the only ones feeling a little disappointed.

Brody took one last glance at Dick's retreating car. "I was looking forward to it."

CHAPTER TWENTY-THREE

"WHO TOLD?" MAE'S eyes narrowed on Brody.

"You know we can't tell you that, Mae." Brett turned to peer down the street. "How long had he been here?"

"Too long." Clara lifted her arm, looking it over for any marks that might have been left by Dick's rough grip. "He won't be back."

"You sure?" Mae tipped the knife in her hand from side to side. "I can get you one of these just in case."

"You can't go around stabbing people, Mae." Boone took a little step toward where Mae stood.

She immediately pointed the blade his direction. "Not people. Probably just you now."

Boone eyed the tip for a second before his blue gaze leveled on the woman staring him down. "You can't stab me with all these witnesses."

"Wrong." She turned to fully-face him. "I can't get away with stabbing you with all these witnesses."

"I didn't see anything." Liza held one hand up, her attention completely focused on her nails.

"You shouldn't stab him." Clara reached out to take the knife from Mae. "Then we'll still have to clean blood off the sidewalk." Clara glanced down. "And I'm not dressed for it."

Mae glared at Boone a second longer. Finally she lifted a shoulder. "He's not worth the effort anyway." She turned and walked into her restaurant, leaving Boone staring after her.

He managed one step toward the door before Brody pushed a hand to the middle of his chest. "Leave her alone, man. You did it once. You can do it again."

Boone's eyes snapped Brody's way. "What the fuck's that supposed to mean?"

"You know damn well what it means." Brody shoved at his brother a little. "You made your choice. Now you have to stand by it and let her be."

Liza's sharp gaze raked down Boone. "She's better off without you anyway."

It was hard not to feel a little bad for Boone. Clara knew what it was like to be punished for the mistakes you made when you were young and stupid.

She just dealt with one of hers.

Liza's eyes stayed on Boone as she followed Mae into the restaurant.

"Seems like you got yourself a fan club, brother." Brett grinned Boone's way.

"Shut up." Boone turned toward his truck. "Come on."

Brett, Brooks, and Boone piled into the still-running vehicle, the engine revving for a second before they pulled away, leaving Clara standing on the sidewalk with Brody.

"You really okay with him signing away his rights to Wyatt?"

Okay was relative. "I wish things could be different." For a while she thought Dick would eventually come around. See what he was missing out on. "But they can't." Clara took a deep breath and let it back out, the air flowing free and easy. "Wyatt deserves to have a father that loves him and appreciates him. Dick was never that."

Brody's lips twitched. "I love that you called him Dick to his face."

"I should have done worse than that." She smiled a little. "But I figured people would think I was crazy if I stood here cussing him out at the top of my lungs." She tried to flatten her smile out. "But now I'm thinking they probably already think I'm crazy for being with you."

"I was hopin' you wouldn't figure that out."

"And what was *that*?" She motioned to the spot where Boone's truck sat just a handful of minutes ago. "What was your plan?"

"We were gonna come kick Dick's ass." He said it like she should have known.

"Looked like you all were pretty well organized." They'd pulled up, parked, and exited the truck before she could even blink her eyes to be sure she was seeing what she thought she was.

"That wasn't our first rodeo, Darlin'." Brody sauntered her way. "I've run a few men out of town in my day."

"A few?" She tipped her head back as he came to stand just in front of her. "Like who?"

"I think that's a story I'll hang onto for a little bit longer." He tipped one finger under her chin. "But I'm sure Mae would be happy to fill you in if you really want to know."

"I thought Mae was going to stab Boone." Having Mae

and Liza at her side bolstered her, made it almost easy to stand up to Dick. Their attitudes were contagious.

"She probably was." Brody wrapped his arms around her, pulling her close. "Thank you for stopping her. The ranch can't handle being down a man right now."

"That's the only reason you're glad she didn't stab him?"

Brody lifted one shoulder. "A little stab might clear all this up so everyone could go on with their lives."

"It wouldn't have been little." Mae stood in the open doorway. She passed over a bag. "I packed up some treats for the kids."

Liza came to the door carrying Clara's purse. "Wanna meet for lunch again next week?"

"You still want to have lunch with me after all that?"

Liza handed Clara her bag. "Are you kidding? We want to have lunch with you *because* of all that."

Clara tried not to smile. "Okay."

"Fantastic." Mae blew her a kiss. "See ya."

"ARE YOU SURE this is what you want to do?" Cliff sounded hesitant.

Like she used to. "Positive."

He sighed into the phone. "Okay. I'll get all the papers mailed out. You'll need to have them notarized and send them back. Then I'll file them with the courts and we should have a date soon."

"Fantastic." Clara hung up, tossing the phone to the bed beside her as she took a deep breath and let it back out.

It was a feeling she couldn't get used to. Breathing without fear of what might come next.

For years that was how she spent her days. Unable to enjoy anything good out of uncertainty and fear.

Always waiting for the other shoe to drop.

It might still drop.

But somehow it didn't seem as scary.

As imposing.

What was Dick going to do? Show up and try to make her agree with him?

He'd done that. And she'd made it through just fine.

"Cla-la?" Michaela peeked around the door frame. "You seeping?"

"I'm not, but you're supposed to be." Clara held her arms out. "What's wrong?"

Michaela raced across the room and launched herself at Clara. "I not tired."

"That doesn't sound right." Clara fell back, taking the toddler with her. "You sure you don't just want to sleep in here?"

Michaela was a master at finding ways to end up taking her naps in the bigger bed in Clara's room.

Clara settled in beside Michaela. "Did you bring a book?"

"Yes I did." Michaela held up her most favorite story. The edges were already worn when Clara came to Red Cedar Ranch. At first she assumed it was from Brody or his mother reading it to her.

Now she knew better.

"This is the story your mommy used to read to you when you were in her tummy." Clara flipped the cover open. "She read you a story every night."

"Mommy loves me." Michaela wiggled down, scooting around until she was perfectly positioned against the pillows.

"That's right. Your mommy loves you." Clara propped her head on one hand as she read the book. It was a short but very sweet story about a chicken who thinks he's a duck in spite of what the other animals on the farm try to tell him. At the end a dip in the farm's pond finally convinces him of the truth.

Usually Michaela belly laughed at the sopping wet chicken deciding he might not be a duck after all.

But this time she was fast asleep before that point came.

Clara slowly stood up, tucking a pillow along Michaela's side before silently creeping down the stairs to where Maryann was in the kitchen, digging through the newest delivery of home decor magazines. Clara sat in one of the chairs lined along the large table. "How's it going?"

"I don't know what I was thinking. I should have never fired that man." Maryann tossed the magazine in her hand to the table before rubbing her eyes. "There's so much to do. I thought I could handle it, but I'm not sure anymore."

She'd been there a hundred times. "All you can do is pick one thing and handle it. Then move on to whatever's next."

Maryann's hands dropped from her eyes and reached across to grab Clara's. "You get things all squared away with that asshole?"

"I think so." She would walk away from the divorce with one thing and one thing only.

It was the only thing of value there was.

"He agreed to sign away his rights and I agreed to the

rest." She took another breath, sure this one would feel like they used to. Tight and anxious and smothered.

It didn't. It came easy and deep.

Because she'd faked it long enough to make it.

"Cliff is sending me the papers. I just have to sign them and send them back and then he can get us a court date so it can be over."

Maryann squeezed her hand. "Good. You and Wyatt need to be free of him."

"I hope Wyatt thinks the same thing." She had done what was best. There was no doubt about it in her mind.

But the worry that Wyatt would suffer from Dick's abandonment still lingered.

"He will be okay either way." Maryann smiled. "He's a smart boy. He understands more than you think."

That was actually what she was worried about.

"The twins should be down for another hour. Is it okay if I go out to the barn for a little bit?"

"Of course, Dear." Maryann huffed out a breath as she picked up the magazine she'd discarded. "I'll be here trying to decide what kind of pillows to order."

Clara stood. "Not down. Some people are allergic."

Maryann pointed her direction. "Smart girl. I might have to make you my picking partner."

"You should get more opinions than just mine." Clara grabbed a few apple chunks from the container she kept in the fridge. "There's more than one interior decorator in the world. Maybe you should hire another one."

"You're right." Maryann stood from the table, shooting her a wink. "Maybe Cliff knows one." Her phone was already pressed to one ear as Clara walked out the back door and headed to the fence.

She whistled.

A few seconds later Edgar poked his head around the side of the stable. The second he saw her the horse started moving a little faster, trotting along the cedar building to where she stood.

"What in the heck have you been rolling in?" His coat was a mess. Covered in dirt and dust and grass and whatever else he'd managed to grind into it. "You think I don't have better things to do than clean you up all the time?"

She'd never had a dog. Not a cat either.

Not even a hamster.

Never in her wildest dreams did she expect to pet a horse, let alone ride one.

Definitely not end up so in love with one.

Edgar dropped his head over the fence, sniffing along what he could reach of her, trying to figure out what she had for him.

Clara held out one of the apples.

"He's going to end up spoiled."

She smiled, keeping her attention on Edgar instead of the cowboy slowly coming her way. "Aren't you supposed to be working?"

"I brought Wyatt back to the house." Brody backed up to the fence beside her. "I think we wore him out."

"He likes it." She wasn't the only one with a fondness for the horses at the ranch.

"He loves it." Brody tipped his head away as Edgar grabbed for his hat.

"He does." Clara passed Edgar another apple to distract

him from his sudden interest in Brody's hat. Edgar checked her out as he chewed through the last of his snack. Once he figured out there was none left he huffed out a sigh and wandered across the grass.

Clara rested her arms over the top of the fence, dropping her chin on them. "Cliff got the papers from Dick's attorney."

"That didn't take long."

Dick clearly wasted no time going back home and getting his attorney to work the new agreement up. One that meant they would be able to fast-track the rest and be done.

Finally.

"He said I should have a date soon."

"So you'll be a single woman again." Brody turned her way. "Bet someone snaps you up so fast it makes your head spin."

"Maybe I'll just stay single forever."

She could barely flatten out a smile as Brody scoffed beside her.

"I knew I shouldn't have told you to hang out with Mae and Liza."

Clara's head fell back as she laughed. "It's too late now."

"It's never too late, Darlin'." Brody eased closer. "Not for anything."

She lifted a brow. "That sounds ominous."

Brody lifted one shoulder. "I don't know that I'd call it ominous." He rested one hand on her back. "But I'm tryin' to pace myself so…"

"Don't even try to lie to me, Brody Pace. You haven't once tried to—"

"I haven't given you the ring I bought you, have I?"

She wanted to glare at him, but it was so damn hard.

No one had ever wanted her the way he did.

Not the father she never knew.

The mother she lost so early in life.

The man she let stifle her into barely existing.

None of them cared about her like Brody did. None of them put her first. None of them pushed her to be strong then held her up while she fought.

But he did.

EPILOGUE

"IT'S SO PRETTY." Clara stood at the newly installed gate, smiling over it in the direction of the only part of The Inn at Red Cedar Ranch that was completed.

Bill Pace eyed the expanse of cement and water. "It should be pretty. It cost an arm and a leg."

Brody's mother slapped his father in the center of the chest. "Hush. It will be worth it."

Brody stared down at the line of small eyes in front of him, wide and eager. "I need everyone to listen to me."

"We listening." Michaela held Clara's hand, swinging it just a little.

"Each of you has to have a grown-up with you at all times." There were enough to go around. It shouldn't be too difficult.

"They get it." Brett lifted his brows. "I'm hot. Let's get a move on."

Brody kept his gaze leveled on the girls. "What's the rule?"

"We will has a grown-up all the times." Michaela repeated his words back with remarkable precision.

"Good." Brody straightened, looking to the other set of eyes on him. "You ready, Little Man?"

Wyatt was practically buzzing with excitement. Had been since they started filling the pool three days ago. His head bobbed in a fast nod. "Yeah."

"Okay." Brody unlatched the gate and pushed it wide. Leah was off and running, racing across the new cement like it was made of hot coals.

"Are you kidding me?" Brody started to run after her, the pile of towels and cooler of snacks he carried slowing him down.

But Leah didn't slow down. She went right on, never hesitating.

Even when she ran out of concrete.

Boone was past him in a flash, racing across the concrete and going straight into the pool. In less than three seconds he was up, a soaking wet Monster coughing in his arms.

"Holy shit." Boone wiped the water from his face. "It's still cold."

"Holy shit." Michaela grinned at her uncle as she said it, loud enough everyone could hear.

Boone shoved a finger Maryann's way as he worked across the shallow end of the pool. "You can't hold that one against me." He pushed back the sagging blonde hair clinging to Leah's face as he scaled the steps. "What happened to staying with a grown-up?"

She gagged, puking a stream of water-thinned hot dog down Boone's bare chest and onto the newly-stained concrete under his feet.

Boone retched, the back of his hand coming to press against his mouth as his stomach worked to free him of its contents. "Someone come take her."

Clara stepped forward, rushing in to scoop Leah up as Boone continued struggling. The minute Leah was passed off Boone turned and rushed toward the new bushes planted around the edge of the pool area, bending at the waist and puking into them.

"Those are new!" Maryann started to run his way, immediately stopping as he heaved again.

"Boone frowin up." Leah watched her uncle with shockingly judgmental eyes.

"Boone is throwing up because you threw up." Brody snagged Leah from Clara, almost gagging himself as the smell of vomit came along with her. "And you threw up because you didn't follow the rules."

"I follow da rules." Michaela stood at Clara's feet. "I'm wif Cla-la."

"I'm going to try to clean her up." Brody turned toward the back door to the inn.

His mother stared at Leah's lost lunch. "My concrete." Her gaze went to where Boone stood, still looking a little green. "My bushes."

Brody carried Leah into the inn, heading straight for the only spot he knew was done enough to be of any use. He stood her on the paper-covered floor and stripped off her suit, rinsing it out in the sink before using the washed suit to wipe her down.

"Here." Clara was at his side with a box of wipes. She pulled a few free and passed them over, taking the suit and giving it a final rinse before wringing it out.

She crouched beside Leah, coming eye-to-eye with the little girl. "You need to go apologize to Uncle Boone. Tell him you're sorry you didn't follow the rules."

Leah's lips pressed into a pout. "Kay."

Clara helped wiggle Leah into her damp suit, finally managing to get it pulled up and into place. "Since you didn't follow the rules you may not go in the pool for ten minutes."

Leah's face puckered up. "Kay, Cla-la."

Clara pulled her in for a hug. "I just want you to always be safe."

Leah sniffed. "I know."

Clara stood, taking Leah's hand in hers. "Let's go tell Uncle Boone you're sorry."

Brody rinsed out the sink as Clara and Leah made their way back outside.

"That would be wonderful." His mother breezed through the door, cell pressed to her ear. Her eyes widened as she saw him.

My sink.

She mouthed the words, rushing over to peer into the stainless steel basin, snagging the sprayer from him. "I am ready whenever you are." Her head snapped up. "Next week?" She looked around the half-finished inn. "Sure. That would be great." A tight smile worked onto her face. "Wonderful. I'll see you then."

She disconnected the call.

"What was that about?"

"I can't believe you got throw up in my new sink." She went back to rinsing away the nothing that was there.

"Did you want me to just let her marinate in it?" Brody

leaned against the counter. "What in the world's got you so wound up?"

Maryann dropped the sprayer, tipping her head back. "This place is making me crazy."

"You're the one who wanted the inn."

His mother's eyes snapped to him. "I know that." She pressed one hand to her head. "I just never expected to run into so many hiccups."

"That's the way it always goes." Brody wiped his damp hands off on the board shorts he wore. "You can't build something like this without running into some issues."

"Some I could handle." She turned toward him, her smile a little less tight. "On the bright side, I think I found a new interior decorator to help me with the rest."

"Good. Cause they can't do anything else until you start picking paint and flooring."

She'd already technically picked everything three times.

It just kept changing.

"And I'm ready to get my place started."

His mother's eyes widened. "Already?"

"Of course already." Brody tipped his head toward the pool. "You think I'm going to risk letting her get away from me?"

His mother ran her hands down the front of the caftan covering her bathing suit. "Well the new decorator is coming Tuesday. Hopefully she's as good as she seems."

He sure hoped so. Aside from wanting to get started on his future with Clara, the ranch needed to start recouping some of the investment currently sitting stagnant.

They had a huge sum wrapped up in the inn, and as nice

as the pool was to have, it was definitely not even close to worth the money.

Brody went back outside, leaving his mother to fret alone.

Clara was stretched out on a lounge chair beside Leah, their hands tucked together as they watched everyone else playing in the water.

Her dark hair fell over one shoulder, shining in the sun. Her black suit was modest in cut, but there was nothing that could hide the lush curves he took every opportunity to worship.

She was the polar opposite of his little blonde-haired daughters. But they were hers none the less. Both found and earned.

"Brody!" Wyatt jumped around in the water between his brothers. "We're playing Marco Polo. Wanna come?"

Right then Brooks lunged at Brett, taking him down hard and fast, both of them going under the water.

Wyatt turned to watch them with wide eyes, slowly backing away as they flailed around, each trying to be the one holding the other one under.

Brody dove in, the cold water more of a shock than he expected. He popped up right beside Wyatt, the chill of the water already seeming to carry less of a bite. Brooks and Brett were still wrestling around, laughing like the idiots they were. Brody backed through the water, heading for a calmer area. "You know how to swim, Little Man?"

Wyatt shrugged. "A little."

"You know how to do a handstand?"

He shook his head.

Brody went into the water head first, finding the bottom

with his hands and pushing up, trying to get his legs as straight as possible. When he came to the top Wyatt immediately went down, managing to do a crooked three second handstand before sliding over.

He came up, wiping his eyes. "Did I do it?"

"You did." Brody held one hand up for a high-five.

Wyatt lunged at him, squeezing him in a tight hug. Brody wrapped his arms around the little boy, squeezing him back.

"I'm proud of you, Buddy."

His eyes met Clara's over the water. She might be all he'd been looking for, but she brought him more than he could have ever imagined.

———

"YOU." CLARA STOOD from where she sat at the edge of Brody's bed and pointed right at his smug face. "Did you think I wouldn't notice what you did?"

She tried to look mad. Did her best to seem upset.

Brody's lopsided grin made it appear she was unsuccessful.

"I don't know what you're talking about."

She whipped up her hand, holding it between them. "I wore this damn thing for an hour before I noticed it was there."

He scoffed. "That's a full carat. How in the hell did you not notice it was there?"

She crossed her arms. "I knew I should have kicked you out before morning."

"Coulda, shoulda, woulda." He gave her a wink. "Who else saw it?"

"You know damn well who else saw it."

Technically Maryann was the first one to see it. Noticed it before Clara slowed down enough to figure out the thing was there.

"Guess you're stuck with it then." He gave her a wink.

"You think I have to marry you because you snuck a ring on my finger while I was asleep?"

"Do *you* think you have to marry me because I snuck a ring on your finger while you were asleep?"

Clara pressed her lips together, fighting the smile he was trying to force on her face.

The man had been hell on wheels since they got back from California. Made it clear where his girls got it from.

"I haven't even been divorced a month."

"Do I look worried about it?" He advanced on her, crossing his bedroom with languid, easy steps.

Brody never looked worried about anything. "What about—"

"Nothing's going to change this, Darlin'." He came closer. "Nothing's going to steal this from you." He shook his head a little, the brim of his hat shading his eyes the same way it had that first day she saw him. "And nothing's going to take you and Wyatt from me." He caught her left hand, his fingers going to the ring she hadn't been able to bring herself to remove. "That's what this is about. Not just you and me. This is about you and me and Wyatt and the girls. All of us." He dropped to his knee, in front of her, dragging her gaze down with him.

Her blood thrummed in her ears, heart racing from something that felt close to panic.

"We are already a family, Clara. This ring doesn't make

that any different." His eyes held hers. "Wear it, don't wear it. That's up to you. But you need to know I'm here for the long haul."

Brody made everything so much more difficult than it had to be.

She could have just come here and been a nanny. She would have had a roof over her head. Money in the bank. Security for her son.

But she would not have had Brody.

And damned if he wasn't worth more than most of the other.

Fake it till you make it.

Jump in with both feet.

Both applied to this situation.

"Fine."

He smiled up at her. The man who proved so much of what she thought she knew wrong.

The man who wanted her.

Wanted her son.

Chose them every time.

Brody turned her palm, pressing a kiss to it, blue eyes steady and sincere.

"Is now the right time to tell you how much I'd love another baby?"

———

Made in United States
Cleveland, OH
22 December 2024